*"Give me an heir within the year,
and Oswin may keep his hands."*

Alys knew she must submit, or the young archer who had rashly risked his life for her would lose his most precious possession . . .

When Sir Geoffrey came to her that night, Alys had been prepared by her old serving nurse. Geoffrey's lips curved a little into an unaccustomed smile. She was so very determined to act the martyr and he was equally determined that this should not be. He tilted up her serious face, and kissed her tenderly. In all the months of marriage he had shown her no gesture of affection, other than the customary kiss of the marriage ceremony. Her body grew icy cold and he saw alarm leap into her eyes. He said no word, but still smiling, gathered her into his arms and moved to the comfort of the bed in which she had slept alone since their marriage night . . .

Amber Promise

Margaret Abbey

Formerly titled

GIRDLE OF AMBER

BALLANTINE BOOKS • NEW YORK

Library of Congress Catalog Card Number: 78-67865

ISBN: 0-345-25421-X

This edition published by arrangement with Robert Hale & Company

Manufactured in the United States of America

First Ballantine Books Edition: February 1979

≈ Chapter One

SIR HUBERT FITZALAN'S forehead creased into a frown as he watched his daughter cross the courtyard with the stirrup cup. Her awkwardness was even more in evidence this morning than usual. Her progress was slow and ungainly, as she limped to his side and reached up to offer him the wine. He thanked her brusquely and drained the tankard in two swallows. His sigh, as he handed it back to her, was long and gusty and she coloured under his scowling scrutiny. He had never loved her mother, in fact the woman had given him little or no pleasure, nothing save a dowry sizeable enough to have allowed him more luxuries for the first year of their marriage. Her greatest fault had been her inability to give him a son, nothing but this plain, crippled daughter, whose appearance now so displeased him. The foolish bitch had had no more sense than to fall heavily with the child in her arms down the stone stair of the keep. True he had pushed her, angered by her entreaty about some matter with which he had not wished to trouble his mind. The child Alys had lived, although she had been ill enough at the time, but her hip was permanently injured they said by the fall, and she would never walk without pain, or ride as other women. Sir Hubert had not been over concerned about that, while there had been a possibility of an heir to succeed him or other daughters more beautiful and eligible to make successful marriages, but his frail young wife had miscarried over child after child but had dragged on a miserable existence until a year ago. He must marry again and provide himself with an heir. There were several rich widows of

1

his acquaintance in Nottingham, and if he could recoup his losses at the tournament, as he hoped, he would doubtless be able to choose the most attractive of their number to succeed Aly's mother. His frown cleared at the thought. The weather was improving; jousting would take place in all the castles and towns of the area. Life would be pleasant again, but he must think while he was away about what was best to be done with Alys.

The girl was standing back now, her brown eyes half closed against the early sun, which was particularly strong for early April, waiting for his last minute instructions. She was obedient enough, anxious to please. Surely he could find some man who would find her an obedient and attentive wife, if not (he pursed his lips at the thought) the nunnery at Rothley would probably be willing to accept her, but first he would try for a marriage settlement. She was yet young, scarcely seventeen. He leaned forward in the saddle, his mailed hand checking his charger's impatient pawing.

"You have my instructions. I shall be back within the month. Leave everything in Gilbert's hands. Curb your tendency to be generous with alms. We can ill afford it. Father Anselm has only to ask and you unloose your purse strings. When I return, I hope to refurbish our coffers. The roofs of the barns need attention. We must look to them later. See to it that the household servants work well."

"I will do as you order, Father." She forced a tired smile. "I wish you success in the jousting. You may leave with a quiet mind. I can manage."

"Aye," he nodded. "You're a good wench. I can trust you. Farewell then." He lifted his hand and the little group of men-at-arms behind him prepared to move forward. The train clattered over the bailey and across the drawbridge. She followed them to the main gate and watched until they were out of sight on the main Nottingham road, then turned back into the bailey again and signalled for the raising of the drawbridge and the lowering of the portcullis. It was unlikely that there would be visitors today and she preferred that they should ask for admittance before entering the courtyards of Birlstone. The castle was ill equipped and poorly manned. It was preferable that any suspicious newcomers should be checked. Cedric, the gatekeeper, was a man to be trusted and he knew the hours when the serfs from the manor were like to come about their business.

Her steps dragged as she moved towards the stair leading to the entrance to the keep. She had been up at dawn attending to the last moment packing arrangements, and the last few days had been a hub-bub of preparation. There was still a great deal to be done. She must visit the kitchens and check on the maids. She had ordered new rushes to be strewn in the hall and it would not be done if she did not herself oversee the task. It was not that the servants were disobedient, rather that they had become lax over the winter months, while her father had spent most of his days hunting or drinking before the smoky fire in the great hall.

When she at last climbed to the solar, Elfrida scolded her and drew her down onto the one chair and lifted her tired limbs onto a stool.

"Lady Alys, you are exhausted. You must not tire your leg so much. You will not sleep tonight for its aching."

"I know, Elfrida, I know, but there was so much to be attended to and father does not think."

"He never thinks." The Saxon woman snorted her disapproval. She hurried to the top of the stair and called for mulled ale. Her mistress seemed chilled. She herself brought the tankard to her and watched as she swallowed.

"You guard me like a dragon," Alys said quietly. "That is good, Elfrida. Thank you. I will rest a little for now. Later I'll work on the tapestry for the hall. It is needed urgently."

"Lady Maude (the Lord bless her) was too ill to give it much of her attention." Elfrida sighed as Lady Alys's dark eyes saddened at the reference to her mother, "But it's no use bemoaning, she's likely at peace now. She had little enough of it in this house."

Alys made no attempt to rebuke the woman for her outspoken criticism of Sir Hubert. She knew well enough how she had loved the frail Norman woman and had served her faithfully since the day she had come to Birlstone as a bride. It was a relief to sit back and rest. There should be no need to eat in the hall tonight. She would get Elfrida to bring her some food here, and eat privately. She could hear the noises from below. Obviously her orders were being obeyed at last. She smiled a little wanly. Perhaps if her father *did* bring a new bride back with him, her tasks would be less arduous. The thought brought with it other disquieting considerations, but she thrust them resolutely aside.

Some commotion from below caused her to sit up in the chair but Elfrida beckoned her authoritatively to sit back and went herself to investigate. She came back some minutes later, her lips tightening with indignation.

"It is Gilbert, lady. He insists on seeing you. I told him you were too tired to be bothered but he has that boy Oswin with him. There's been some trouble in the woodland of the demesne. It is the boy who pleads to see you."

"Send them up."

"But my lady . . ."

"Do as I say, Elfrida, please." She softened the imperiousness of the command by smiling and touching the older woman's hand comfortingly, and shaking her head in disapproval, Elfrida clattered down the stairs.

Gilbert, her father's bailiff, was a thin ferrety faced man. Alys found his obsequiousness distasteful, but her father trusted the man and she greeted him courteously. Her gaze went from him to the thirteen-year-old boy, who despite every effort to prevent him, rushed to her side and fell to his knees by her chair.

"Please, Lady Alys, don't let them. They will cripple her, my Hella—she meant no harm."

"Lady, the boy has been told time after time that the

wolfhound bitch was not to enter the game preserves.
They were both there this afternoon knowing your father to be away, they took the opportunity to poach.
And the boy was armed." Gilbert indicated the bow
over the boy's shoulder. "In any case he should have
been working on his land. Since his father died, there is
plenty to be done and he will be behindhand with his
share of work on the demesne."

"What have you to say, Oswin?" Alys's voice was
stern, but she touched his red head in a partial caress.
She had a fondness for the sturdy Saxon lad, who carried the full responsibility of a large family since his father had died almost two years ago.

He hung his head and was silent. She prompted him
gently, "Well?"

"I did go into the woods, lady. I know I should not
have done but I killed nothing. I shot only at targets I
had set up, truly. I was practising for the archery contest next month in Nottingham. Hella did not touch the
game, I swear it."

"You know the forestry laws, Oswin, well enough. If
Hella attacks the game, she must be lamed."

"But she did not, Lady Alys."

"I think this time we can afford to be generous, Gilbert." She looked up directly at the frowning bailiff. "I
know you think I am challenging your authority but I
believe the boy's story. I have seen him around with
the bitch. I am convinced that he can control her. I
will see that he makes up his lost time. You may leave
us."

The bailiff had no excuse to argue further. He
bowed stiffly and withdrew. The boy rose and backed
away a little.

"I shall never forget, Lady Alys. Hella means so
much to me but I would give her to you if . . ."

"No, no, Oswin. She would fret for you. Take her
with you, but if you would keep her safe she must stay
out of the parkland."

"I know it." He flushed with gratitude. "When she
whelps, I will give you a puppy."

"I would like that."

"It would guard you well, better than those grey-hounds Lady Matilda at Thorpe has."

"I don't doubt it. Hella looks formidable enough to frighten the most challenging foe. You will recall what I said. I cannot keep saving you from Gilbert's displeasure and if my father should hear of your misdemeanour. . . ."

"I know it, lady. I will remember."

"Then leave me, Oswin, for I am very tired." He bowed awkwardly and she heard him take the keep steps at a clumsy run and whistle to the wolfhound bitch at their foot. She looked up at Elfrida's stern face and coaxed her to smile.

"He is too young for sorrow, Elfrida. Do not scold me."

"And your back is too frail to carry your father's anger. That Gilbert will carry tales."

"Like enough. He does not like me, Master Gilbert. However, he is reliable enough and I cannot complain of his ability, nor is he excessively cruel to the serfs."

"Aye, like enough. He knows how to tread the line. Look out for him, if there is ever an opportunity to cheat you with impunity."

Alys looked up at her shrewdly but Elfrida's head was bent over her portion of the tapestry, and it was evident that she would get no more from her on the subject.

The days followed each other with regular monotony. Work on the manor was proceeding smoothly and with Sir Hubert away, Alys found life less exhausting. He was not able to demand her presence in the great hall or in the courtyard, bellowing her name as he was wont to do, all over the castle, when he wanted some trifling object or refreshment. She was able to organise the work to a simple routine and her leg ached less, since she was not forced to mount the stairs of the keep so many times.

When Father Anselm called to say mass in the chapel, he stayed to eat with her afterwards. The fat little priest was kindly and she enjoyed his companionship and valued his advice. "Your father will be long away?" he enquired, wiping his greasy fingers on the cloth a man held for him, at the close of the meal.

"He said about a month but I think it will be longer. He goes courting."

"Indeed?" The bushy brows met in an arch of enquiry.

"He needs an heir. It is obvious." She shrugged and smiled suddenly. She had a pleasing smile, he thought, it illuminated her whole face. If the girl frowned less and took life more easily she would be comely enough. Certainly, she was no beauty. Her hair was brown and undistinguished, her complexion good and her light golden brown eyes candid and large. They were perhaps her one beauty, though her nose was straight enough, but the face was too square and the mouth too wide for the usual standards of feminine beauty. As she sat opposite to him, reposing in the chair, her figure was slender and attractive. It was such a disadvantage that when she rose to move, her clumsiness stirred pangs of sudden pity.

"And what does he propose to do about you?" he questioned gently.

"I do not know, Father." Her lip trembled a little while the smile remained but became a little frosty, "I am not shaped for marriage."

"Nonsense, you will make some man a fine wife."

"But who, Father? He must be willing to accept me first."

"If your father put out some feelers and took you into County society more, you would not lack for suitors. Men do not marry for love, my child, but sensibly for companionship and an ability to make a good chatelaine."

"And for children."

"We do not know of any reason that would prevent you having a family."

"I think not but first a man must desire me enough to take me to bed."

"My child, that is true but you talk as if you were ugly and deformed, this is not so."

"I am not straight."

"It is the will of God, Alys. You must not be bitter."

"I know that, Father. It is not I who recriminate. Perhaps," she hesitated and looked at him directly, "perhaps it is the will of God that I should dedicate myself to his service."

"Enter a nunnery?" He pursed his lips. "It is a hard life, child."

"You think me unfit? I can work hard."

"Truly child I was not thinking of that."

"Then why . . ."

"Give yourself time. The convent walls should only enclose those who have a true vocation. I am not at all sure that it is the life for you."

There was no more to be said at that time and she wisely decided to wait for a more favourable opportunity to broach the matter which was most troubling her heart.

As Father Anselm had remarked, Alys lived a lonely life at Birlstone. Her father had been the only son, and there were no close relatives on either side to pay her calls. Sir Hubert had not found it convenient to take his daughter to either of the nearby towns of Leicester or Nottingham, and indeed she found it excessively tiring to do so, being unable to ride, and she was forced to travel in a litter which was not easy on her cramped limbs and caused increased aching of the right hip. She knew no women of her own age with whom she could gossip, and as her mother had been ailing most of her life, she had found Elfrida, her nurse attendant, her only confidante. She was content enough as the Spring days lengthened, and by late May, her father had not returned home. He had sent her brief messages from a man-at-arms. He was finding Nottingham entertaining and had taken a quantity of money in ransom and two chargers which would fetch a good price at the market. He charged his daughter to keep matters running smoothly while he was away, but further than that, he gave her no news. Gilbert came regularly to make his reports and during the lengthening evenings, she and Elfrida sat companionably, working on the new tapestry for the hall.

It was late in the afternoon of the last Saturday of May and she was crossing the courtyard after visiting the smithy, when she was surprised to see her father's captain, Walter, ride in a puther of dust across the drawbridge. His face was grim as he dismounted and seeing her unexpectedly close, he checked in his stride, before coming to her side.

"What is it, Walter, something wrong in Nottingham?"

"Aye, lady."

"My father, he has sent me a message?"

"No, lady." The man was clearly uncomfortable and she checked her rising impatience. The castle retainers knew well enough how her father treated her, and in their rough way, gave her evidence of their unspoken sympathy. If her father had now sent her some ill tempered order, it would be hard for Walter to bring himself to deliver it. She waited quietly and he turned back to look full into her troubled brown eyes.

"Please tell me, Walter. Whatever he has decided, I can bear it."

"It is ill news, lady. You must prepare yourself."

So he had chosen a bride and had bidden her prepare.

Walter's embarrassment was due to his understanding of her reluctance to relinquish her authority, but she had expected it.

Her father was a young man. His remarriage sooner or later was a certainty, yet when the news came, she did not at once comprehend and could only stand staring at him, dry-eyed and stony of features.

"Your father was killed, lady. It was yesterday at the tournament. Prince John is in residence at the castle and the jousts were held in his honour. Your father was confident of success. It was in the mêlée. He was knocked from his horse and the force of the fall broke his back. He had become over-heavy of late, or so the little Jewish physician said."

His voice came to her from a distance. He droned on, giving her detail after detail; how they had tried to help him, but he had been killed at once, they thought. She recovered herself as his voice became crisper, as he explained what had been decided.

"They are bringing him home, lady, on a bier. The cortège should reach Birlstone by nightfall. I rode on to give you the news."

By now a little group of people had gathered behind her and Elfrida gathered the stricken girl to her breast.

"There, lady, come inside. Let yourself weep in peace."

She pulled herself together and heard herself giving instructions. "Prepare to lay the master in the chapel. Put up trestles. One of you, go for Father Anselm. It is all right, Elfrida, I shall be calm. Later will be the time for weeping. Thank you, Walter. I am sure all was done that could be done. Go now and rest. I must go in and think what needs to be done." She hardly heard the mutter of voices as she passed up the steps of the keep and into the kitchens. She still felt very dazed, but not enough to not realise fully the blow which had fallen. Later would be the time to think of herself. Now she must take full charge as the castle's chatelaine.

During the days of mourning, she found herself unable to show grief. The shock had bereft her of thought. As she watched Father Anselm during the requiem, she could only think that it could not be her noisy, blustering, jovial father who lay there so still. He had not even been in a state of grace. Death had overtaken him so hurriedly, in the full flush of his hopes. He had expected to bring home a wealthy and attractive bride and instead he would be soon beside the frail woman he had so despised.

The little priest had been very gentle in his comforting. "It was how he would have liked to have died, doing what he enjoyed," he said quietly and she nodded abstractedly. Her father's wishes were no longer her concern. What would happen to the castle? By the law of the land, it would pass to the crown, since there were no male heirs and the King himself must make provision for her. Sooner than she had thought, it would be time to become a bride of Christ.

Two days later, she sent for Father Anselm and he found her sitting quietly in her little alcove off the great hall which she had turned to a solar for her own use. Deep mourning had not enhanced her plain features, but she seemed calm enough.

"Father Anselm, I am sorry to trouble you, but this came some hours ago, and as you know there is no one in the castle to read it for me. It came from Nottingham from one Baron Geoffrey de Courcelles by one of his men-at-arms. Do you know of him?"

The priest seated himself at her waved invitation and took the sealed letter. "Not that I recall at the moment, my child. We will see what he says. Doubtless it is some message of sympathy from a companion of your father's."

She inclined her head while he broke the seal and gave his attention to the letter. He paused and lifted his shrewd little face to hers, sharply.

"Did the man-at-arms give you any idea of its contents, lady?"

"No, he seemed a grave, reserved man. He presented it and I sent him to the guard room to rest. What does he say?"

"He sends sympathy to you in your loss, the usual conventional phrases then . . ." he broke off, his eyes troubled, but her questioning expression demanded an answer and he swallowed and continued. "He goes on to say that he is charged by Prince John with the defence of the castle and that he will be here on Friday after he has made various arrangements."

"I see, the prince has been quick. I expected it, but not so soon. He does not trust William de Lacey who is Robert FitzParnel's retainer at Mountsorrel. We will have to make preparations to leave. Perhaps Mother

Superior at Rothley would take me in for a while, do you think that best, Father?"

The priest was silent for a moment then he folded the parchment and looked up at her. "That is not all he says, my child."

"Not all—there is something else?"

"He instructs you to prepare to wed him as soon after his arrival as possible. He informs you that since you are a ward of court and under the protection of the crown, the King being away, his brother, Prince John as Regent, formally gives you in marriage to the Baron and with you, your castle, lands and possessions."

✸ Chapter Two

FATHER ANSELM shook his head at the sight of the two large chests in the entrance room. When Alys appeared at the top of the stair she was cloaked for a journey. Elfrida stood behind her laden with further articles of clothing. The kitchen servants were silent as she descended and the greasy young scullion wiped away a dirty tear from his cheek with his bared arm.

"You are determined then?" the priest's voice was concerned.

"Mother Superior has promised me sanctuary. Walter will escort me in the litter. I can be there by noon."

"Could you not at least wait a little?"

"For what? Father Anselm, you cannot expect me to submit to this."

"My child it is the Regent's command. Even the convent cannot hold you close against his wish."

"No one would break sanctuary."

"Child, there are ways and means to compel obedience."

Alys came quietly to his side. "I know, Father, you are concerned for the villagers, but this man will need workers. He will not wreak his anger on them. You cannot ask me to wait and see his face . . . when he first catches sight of me. My lands are what he desires, nothing else. If I enter the nunnery, they can be his."

"I am not happy about your decision. While the King is absent, Prince John is all powerful. If he wishes you to marry this man, he can enforce his will. It may not be such an ill match. You will be provided for."

"Dear Father Anselm, I know you want nothing but my happiness." She paused, as suddenly the sound of a horn came clearly across from the village. It was imperious, clear, demanding. It was unlikely to be the retainers of William de Lacey so far from his own land. She shivered a little. She had heard a great deal of this man, and none of it to his credit. Her escort to Rothley could only be small as the new master would expect to see the castle well defended on his arrival. She was determined not to fear during the journey, though it was not beyond the bounds of possibility that she might be attacked and held to ransom. At this moment she was a wealthy enough heiress. Elfrida opened her mouth to expostulate but she silenced her with a look. "You know my mind, Elfrida. You have my permission to stay if you wish to do so."

"Lady, you know I will not leave you."

"Then let us go to the courtyard."

She moved awkwardly to the door, after first speaking a quiet farewell to the servants, then frowned as she heard further evidence of the nearness of a company of men; the jingle of harness, snorting of horses and the harsh note of command. Gilbert, the bailiff, agitatedly thrust his way into the room and spoke breathlessly. He had mounted the keep steps at a run.

"My lady, the Baron has arrived. He awaits entry to the courtyard. Did you not hear his horn?"

"The Baron de Courcelles, but it is not yet noon."

"My lady, if he mounted at dawn it would not be impossible."

"Tell the men to admit him and his party." She faltered for a moment. What was she to do now that the unexpected had happened? She turned anxiously towards Father Anselm for guidance. He shook his head and gestured to her quietly to go outside to greet the new lord of the manor. She felt there was indeed nothing else she could do.

From the top of the keep steps, she watched his arrival. He was mailed and behind him rode a company of men-at-arms, about thirty in all. His squire carried his banner behind him. It floated free in the wind, a golden gryphon rampant on a field of azure. She descended the steps and he dismounted and came towards her. She had not known what to expect. He wore no helmet and had thrust back his mailed coif clear from his head, and she saw that he was unexpectedly fair, the hair cut in a short thick fringe onto his forehead to take the weight of the helmet. He was tall and broad and she was glad that for this greeting she remained standing on the third step from the ground, or she would have been dwarfed by him. She judged him to be about twenty three or four years of age, with a broad Breton face, stern and unyielding and wide direct blue eyes which seemed to look at, and beyond her.

"Lady Alys FitzAlan?" He paused about three feet from the keep and removed his mailed gauntlet to greet her.

She inclined her head, her mouth a little dry, but forced herself to greet him.

"I am indeed. You will be Sir Geoffrey de Courcelles. I am charged by the Prince to give you welcome, Sir. Will you not give your men leave to dismount?"

He signalled briefly, and the men dismounted quietly and stood waiting, checking their mounts' impatient pawing and stamping. She stood back, but he motioned her to precede him into the keep.

"You are cloaked for a journey, lady?" His question

was challenging and she saw his blue eyes sweep round the entrance room to the clutter of chests and packages, stacked ready for her departure.

She coloured. The situation was embarrassing in the extreme.

"I had planned to go to the nunnery at Rothley for a while," she said stiffly.

His straight fair brows arched into a question and as he was silent, she felt impelled to give an explanation, "I thought it best until—until I had a chance to think things over."

"Indeed." His stern mouth curved into a wry smile. "I had not thought to see the daughter of Sir Hubert FitzAlan fly the field before engaging the enemy."

"There was no such thought in my mind, sir."

"But you did not intend to be here to greet me."

She turned to face him conscious of the high colour flaming her cheeks. "Sir Knight, I felt it better that you were told fairly of my disability."

"I was not unaware of it." His gaze swept over her tense little body, balanced now with one foot forward, to make more comfortable her stance, the right leg being slightly shorter. "I am not dissatisfied with what I see. Come, Lady Alys, we are neither of us children. We dispensed with the romantic notions the minstrels sing about, years ago. The Regent has commanded me to wed you and control the castle, and the idea is practical enough. I am no idle young gallant. My mind is taken up with military affairs. My mother has frequently urged me to marry. You seem a sensible girl. Even here, I see evidence that you are a competent chatelaine and will make me an excellent wife."

She lifted her chin a trifle aggressively. "You take little account of my feelings in the matter, Sir Knight."

"You have a romantic attachment? I was told it was not so."

She was furious that her virgin state should have been discussed in Nottingham and felt inclined to give a sharp answer, but she was interrupted by the en-

trance of Sir Geoffrey's captain-at-arms who paused
uncertainly in the doorway.

"Well?" Sir Geoffrey's curt enquiry cut short his momentary loss of attention, as he peered curiously at his
commander's intended bride.

"Your pardon, sir. The rear column has now joined
the main party. They have brought the prisoner."

"Prisoner—I don't understand?" Alys turned questioning eyes on the Baron.

He shrugged, "We were attacked as we came
through the hazel thicket. A red headed boy shot at
me. The arrow missed me, but I would not say he was
a poor marksman. It was near enough. My horse
reared. I could have been unseated."

"A red-head you say? Then it was Oswin."

"Yes."

"One of your serfs?"

"Yes."

The captain remained at attention. "The men wish
to know if they are to break ranks and seek quarters,
Sir."

"Of course. See to it. The horses must be rubbed
down and stabled. Choose twelve good men beside
yourself to sleep in the hall, the rest can be accom-
modated in the guard huts in the bailey. They will be
overcrowded, but it will suffice for the present. Later
we must extend the outbuildings."

"And the boy, Sir?"

"Hang him." He slipped off his other gauntlet and
moved carelessly to the fire-place.

Alys impelled herself forward, and touched his arm.

"No—please, I pray you."

He turned, surprised at her touch. "You have a
fondness for the boy? Forgive me, I did not consider. I
would not for the world displease you. Do not distress
yourself. Roul take the boy to the guard house, blind
him and let him go."

"Oh no—" horror stung her to an alarmed cry and
again his level brows were raised in an arch of polite
surprise.

"Madam," he said quietly, "I ask you to recall that the lad attempted to kill me and almost succeeded. You must allow that I am entitled to some measure of protection. The boy is a good archer. If he is not maimed, he could become a potential danger."

She swallowed and nodded her head. He had right on his side. Her father would not have hesitated for a moment, yet she was forced to try her best for the boy.

"Sir Geoffrey, the boy did this for me."

"Madam," the word expressed incredulity and she plunged on. "You must not think that I—I have done him some favours in the past and he felt he owed me a debt of gratitude."

"Which he intended to repay, by ridding you of me. You must have made your distaste extremely public, Lady Alys."

"Indeed I did not," she replied swiftly. "I would not dream of discussing a matter of such importance in the hearing of serfs. The boy overheard some gossip obviously and attempted to save me from what he thought was an ill fate. The boy is impetuous."

"So I have noticed." He smiled thinly and moved away to peer up to the gallery which gave access to the slitted windows of the first floor of the keep. He considered their condition and she knew that he was already planning the position of his archers in the event of attack. As he had made no further remarks on the subject of the boy's fate, she turned appealingly to Father Anselm. He shook his shoulders gently, implying helplessness, and she sought quickly words to soften the baron's heart. It did not appear that one interrupted Sir Geoffrey de Courcelles when he was deep in thought.

He turned back suddenly and smiled again. "As you wish, Lady Alys. Take him away, Roul. I will consider with you later what will disable the boy most humanely. Leave us now."

"He may keep his eyes?"

"I have said that I have no wish to anger you. It shall be as you desire."

"Thank you." She drew back, high colour again flooding her face and throat.

He stood with his back to the fireplace and nodded in acknowledgement as his captain-at-arms saluted him and withdrew. —

"You understand your own people naturally. It will help if you can give me information about them."

"You mean that if I agree to marry you, you will be kinder to my people."

Again he smiled and shook his head. "No, that was not what I meant. You overrate your powers of persuasion. It is natural that your people know you, and desire the inheritance to pass to your children. They will be less rebellious, if that is so. They will have you to listen to their problems and to plead for them in the manor court. It is as simple as that."

She went from him to the doorway, and stared bleakly out over the bailey. The strange men-at-arms in their blue livery were bustling about, unpacking, stabling the horses and finding accommodation. Her servants stood in a little knot, sullenly watching them. It was as he had said. There was none to watch over them but herself. She thought with an icy pang of the red-headed boy who had foolishly attempted to help her. There would be others. For their sake, she must make a wise decision. He made no effort to hurry her, and when at last she turned back into the hall, he continued to wait silently. There was a quality of stillness and quiet efficiency in him, she had known in no other man. Her father had been a blustering bully, before whom she often trembled in fear of physical ill treatment. She had a different dread of this man, yet he was courteous enough.

"I will wed you, Sir Geoffrey," she said at last quietly, "when and where you will."

"There is a priest here. Have you a chapel?"

She nodded. "It is very small and bare. It is off the great hall."

"Excellent, then, Father, I suggest you wed us today. I regret that you will miss the chance to air your finery in company, Lady Alys, but that is impossible while you are in mourning for your father. Later we will give a feast and entertain our neighbours. What do you say?"

"Whatever you think best, sir."

"So be it. If you will excuse me I will attend to the settling of my men, and change into more suitable attire. A simple ceremony in two hours say, then perhaps you can provide a meal."

"My bailiff will attend to the details. You will wish to have my father's room?" Her question was somewhat hesitant.

"Your parents had private apartments?"

"Yes," she lowered her head, angry that betraying colour should again flood her features. "Behind the great hall."

"Then they shall be ours, certainly. If your bailiff will escort me, I will give you some privacy, Lady Alys."

"I will send for Gilbert." She curtseyed and he bowed gravely as she withdrew with Elfrida to her own tiny solar. Father Anselm excused himself and went off to prepare the chapel. His brow was creased in bewilderment and he could only pray the Virgin that he had offered Lady Alys the right counsel.

Elfrida was inclined to chatter but Alys silenced her with a gesture. She was very close to tears and she could not bear the woman's idle speculations now. She slipped off her black dress and donned her best kirtle and overtunic of dark blue linen. It was simple and decent enough for her mourning, and she could not stand beside Sir Geoffrey in homespun wool. Elfrida let down her thick brown hair and combed it till it hung down her back in shining waves, then at her request, she left her. Alys knelt at her prie-dieu and prayed to the Virgin for guidance. She was tired of worry and problems, of arguments and the need for explanations. Fate had provided her with the husband she had never expected to acquire. She must do her best to please him and organise the castle for his comfort. In time her strangeness would become respect. Many women she knew would envy her this tall fair stranger, who was not old or ugly or fat or ill mannered. It was just that she felt she might have understood him better if he had indeed been more as she might have expected.

Alys remembered little of the ceremony which made her Lady Alys de Courcelles. Vaguely she recalled repeating the phrases which Father Anselm prompted her to say, and then was conscious of the cold feel of the gold signet ring her new husband placed on each of her fingers as he repeated, "In the name of the Father, the Son, and the Holy Ghost, Amen." It was too large and weighty for third finger of her left hand, where it remained on the "Amen" and he commented afterwards that he must summon a goldsmith to fit it more carefully. Father Anselm blessed them at the entrance to the chapel where their people could witness the final act, from the great hall.

She could not have said afterwards what she ate. The food was well prepared and served but it appeared tasteless. She remembered hearing snatches of his conversation with Father Anselm and she found herself answering his polite questions mechanically. Her servants had obviously done their best to please her and afterwards she visited the kitchen with her new lord to congratulate them. As there was no minstrel present, or entertainers, it seemed pointless to linger in the hall. He acknowledged her request to be excused to the privacy of their apartment and she left him talking to the priest.

Elfrida was surprisingly silent as she prepared her for bed. Standing in her shift, Alys shivered suddenly, though the weather was mild, it being early summer. Her father's chamber, which he had shared with her frail, frightened mother, seemed unfamiliar and unwelcoming, though the bed of carved oak was one of the few treasures they possessed. It had come with her great-great grandfather who had followed Duke William from Normandy. Elfrida held up the scratched iron mirror for her to briefly scrutinise her face. It swam wraithlike in the grey metal reflection, as if it were the face of a stranger. She thanked her maid gravely and slid naked into the large bed. Elfrida had drawn fresh linen sheets from the dower chest and they perfumed the room with the scent of the rose petals and lavender which had been placed among the folds. She slid back and watched the light fade from the high slit of the window. Elfrida smiled down at her.

"I wish you joy, my lady. It was what we all wanted for you. A fine strong husband."

"Thank you." She forced a tired smile and clasped the maid's hand just once and gestured her to leave her alone.

She could hear the sounds from the hall below. The men were settling in their new quarters. When he came to her side, his voice was unemotional.

"Do not fear, Lady Alys. I have no intention of forcing my attentions on you, until we at least know one another somewhat better. It seemed wiser to marry at once. Indeed there was no reason for delay, but there will be plenty of time to become acquainted with each other's dispositions. For the present, I am content if you continue to act as chatelaine and instruct me in the customs of the manor." He smiled down at her. "I will sleep here, otherwise it would excite comment. You will not be afraid?"

She shook her head and he turned from her to the other side of the room where his squire had unpacked his clothing and placed them in her father's chest. She lay silent until she heard his quiet even breathing at her side and at last forced her tired brain to relax and allow her to sleep also.

~~ Chapter Three

THE FIRST fog of November shrouded Birlstone and Alys shivered by the smoky fire in the hall. She unclasped her warmest cloak and Elfrida took it from her, clicking her tongue in the familiar disapproving manner Alys knew well. She moved towards the blaze and held out her hands to feel the warmth, for the moment determined to hold off her maid's censures. She did not need Elfrida to tell her that she would suffer for her foolhardiness in venturing forth in such weather. Her hip was already giving excruciating pain, which she knew augured a sleepless night, but it had seemed important that she check that the work on the barn roof had been completed properly and that the new stabling was adequate. With Sir Geoffrey away, it was essential that she did not allow the servants to become slack. She gave instructions to Gilbert about the evening meal and sank down for a moment before continuing up the next flight of steps to her private apartment. She was too wearied to try that yet. At last it was all done and she could rest by the fire in her own room and allow Elfrida to cosset her to her satisfaction.

Looking back over the past few months she marvelled at what had been achieved. Sir Geoffrey had been tireless in his determination to make the castle impregnable and also more comfortable. He had inspected the stores below and declared them inadequate. The Autumn slaughter had been the busiest time, followed by the salting and hanging of the winter meat. Beside this he had insisted on extra grain being stored as well as plentiful supplies of fruit and cheeses. Fortunately the harvest had been good this year. The well had needed attention, a primary necessity in case they were besieged, and all walls had been inspected and repaired. More outbuildings had been constructed in the bailey and the men were now more comfortably quartered. Even then he had not been satisfied and pressed ahead with the repairs and building of the stables and barns.

During the whole of this time he had treated her with courteous consideration. On recalling the days when she had wept with weariness and despair of ever pleasing her father, she realised she had never been so fortunate. He left no decisions to her, but nevertheless she had felt anxious to work as hard as she could to assist him. She was conscious that though his wife in name, she could not in reality claim that position. If he had a physical need of her or any woman, he had shown no sign of it. Now he was away in Winchester, summoned by Prince John to council, and if he had showed a desire for the company of some pretty companion, she would not blame him in her heart. His kindness to her was apparent, but she still walked in awe of him, as she knew did all his own men, and the fear of displeasing him soon affected the rest of her own serfs. He was stern and unyielding, considerate but inflexible. She smiled a little as she thought of his dealing with Oswin.

The morning after her wedding had been a difficult one. He had left her side early to return to his men, and when she joined him later, he had made a hearty breakfast, after enquiring civilly if she had slept well.

Oswin had come to her, shame-faced and chastened. He had knelt by her chair and touched her knee with his lowered red head.

"The Baron says you are to regard me as his first present, my lady," he had said awkwardly.

She had lifted his chin and stared into his grey eyes, "You are not hurt?"

"No, lady. My shoulders are sore, that is all."

"Oswin, whatever prompted you to do so foolish an

act? You are fortunate not to hang from the highest oak in the parkland—you know that?"

"I know it, lady, and I know it is due to your pleading. He has told me how you begged him not to blind me, and he sends me to you, completely whole, only," he swallowed and she waited for him to continue, ". . . only I am never to carry a bow again. If he sees me armed so, once more, he has sworn to take my right hand."

It had proved a just punishment but a hard one. Oswin had hoped to become champion archer of the locality. He spent hours practising when not toiling on his strips, or on the lord's land, and this put paid to all hopes of ever proving his skill at the local archery contests at Leicester and Nottingham. She had felt sorry for him, but the penalty was well deserved.

Over the months the boy's attitude towards his new lord had been one of grudging respect. He had worked hard and appeared to hold no grudge. His fanatical devotion to Alys pressed him to give loyalty to the man who was now her husband, but she smiled to herself sometimes as she knew the boy watched carefully for any sign of her new lord's cruelty towards her or lack of respect. Since he had found none, he had given his allegiance and she was relieved. The boy's welfare had ever concerned her.

Her reverie was disturbed by the sudden entrance of her captain at arms, Walter. He seemed a little concerned, so she called him at once to her side. The man was utterly trustworthy. It was for this reason that Sir Geoffrey had left him in charge and taken his own captain, Roul, with him to Winchester.

"What is it, Walter? You look worried."

"Lady, four strangers are seeking admittance."

"At this hour—strange," she raised her eyebrows as surprised as he. All day the fog had persisted. It was a typical late Autumn day when every shrub and tree in the park dripped water. Cold clammy fingers of fog ate into the bones and the roads were already becoming difficult of impasse, churned as they were in places into

a morass of claying mud and slime. It was not the
weather for hunting. All the serfs would be huddling
already round their meagre fires before the hour of
curfew when they would be forced to extinguish them.
Certainly she had expected no visitors and therefore
shared in part Walter's disquiet. "Strangers you say?"

He nodded. "Strangers indeed, outlandish I'd call
them."

"I do not understand."

"One of them is a foreigner. He has a dark beard
and has gold jewels in his ears. He says he has been
sent by Sir Geoffrey. The others are servants of his, I
gather."

"There are four you say?" she smiled suddenly
despite her weariness. "They can hardly outnumber
our armed force. Admit them, Walter, and send the
one who appears to be in authority to me, here."

He gazed at her doubtfully, then bowed slightly and
withdrew. She waited in some curiosity for her visitor
to be admitted. Even so, she had not expected to greet
the man who paused in the entrance, then came forward and swept her a low elaborate bow in Eastern
fashion, his swarthy fingers touching his forehead,
bearded lips and breast. He was small and very slender, clad from head to foot in a loose flowing garment
of embroidered scarlet velvet, wet and begrimed now,
but of obvious splendour. His silver turban was clasped
with a large red jewel which glowed with a dull, yet
fiery lustre and two lively black eyes appraised her,
over bearded mouth and chin. He was of middle age,
possibly about forty years or even older, since his
movement and gesture showed an odd bird-like and
quaint vigour which she judged he would carry to his
grave. His English was perfect but oddly accented and
not unattractive, despite its harshness.

"Lady, I despaired of reaching you before nightfall.
My apologies for disturbing you at such a late hour. I
have been charged by Baron Geoffrey de Courcelles,
your husband, to wait upon you, to deliver his message
and to give into your hands various presents he wishes

to give you. We started early this morning from Coventry but the weather worsened and we lost our way. Indeed I feared the necessity of remaining in some wood for the night, but since I am used to warmer climes, as you see for yourself, I was relieved to hear from a yoeman in the village nearby, that I was nearer to Birlstone than I had thought."

"Since you have come from Winchester, I bid you welcome, Sir."

Again he made her the low, sweeping foreign bow, almost an obeisance. "Forgive me. I have not even now fully explained my presence. I am Ibrahim ben Echtal and I am blessed with the friendship of your husband."

"A Saracen?"

"Truly, lady, but no infidel. I am a Christian and for this reason, I am here in this inclement country."

Alys gestured him to the fire, politeness compelling her to restrain her obvious curiosity. "Remove your wet outer garments, Sir, and draw closer to the blaze. My bailiff will deal with your servants and see to the arrangements of the baggage."

He swept off the outer cloak, revealing a long robe of matching scarlet velvet beneath, ornamented only by a long gold chain which almost reached to his waist. He waited until she had seated herself and she felt his shrewd black eyes watch her carefully as she did so, then he himself sat down on an oaken stool and held out jewelled fingers to the warmth.

"I trust you will excuse my apparent rudeness, lady, if I suggest that as soon as possible you retire to your apartment. You are not well."

She flushed hotly. "You are kind, Sir, but I could not leave a guest to eat alone in the hall on the first night of his stay."

"Indeed, lady, you may do so without fear of offending me. I omitted to explain that I am a physician and I counsel you to do so in your best interests."

"A physician?" She looked puzzled and he explained.

"My story is a long and complicated one and I will not bore you with the details. I was born in Damascus and it was there I encountered Sir Geoffrey when he attended the King for a while, after the siege of Acre. I was captured and he treated me with kindness and civility. In return I was able to treat some of his men and attended him too, when he suffered a tertian fever. I am a Christian as I told you and chose to accompany him at his suggestion when he returned to England. I enjoy his protection and have recently lived for a while in a castle on the Welsh marches, Gwyndd. Since joining him at Winchester, he requested that I precede him here and await his return. He hopes to spend Christmas at Birlstone, but cannot be sure of doing so."

"You appear to be a man of many parts, Ibrahim ben Echtal." He bowed gracefully, his eyes dancing.

"I am a teller of tales, a good judge of precious stones and horseflesh, an indifferent soldier, but my skill at bone-setting and the compiling of medicines has been my principle asset. Allow me to prescribe for you tonight. You are in pain. Is it not so?"

She nodded. "My hip aches. The wet aggravates the old injury and I know I shall get little sleep. I have overtired the limb. Please do not concern yourself. This state is quite common. I shall be well enough in a few days."

"But your health *is* my concern. You are Sir Geoffrey's lady. One of my duties is to attend his family and household. Please call your woman and retire. Your servants will provide for me. Can you assign me a small room somewhere, where I can sleep and concoct my drugs and medicines?"

"But of course. I will instruct Gilbert to screen off one of the alcoves of the hall above. There is one quite large one and it can be made comfortable for your use."

"I thank you, and now, please summon your attendant, and obey me."

It was bliss to allow Elfrida to put her to bed with a heated brick, wrapped in wool, at her feet. She had been too wearied to argue and the little physician took charge in a surprising way, ordering her servants and giving instructions for the storing of three large chests which he had brought with him. She ate a little of the meal Elfrida brought from the hall and was relieved to hear that her guest had eaten well and had appeared at ease.

Elfrida admitted him later, when he brought her a goblet of rather bitter liquid which he requested that she swallow.

"It is unpleasant, Lady Alys, but will give you relief. I swear it will do you no harm, but allow you to sleep peacefully and without pain."

She looked up at his dancing black eyes and obeyed him without a word. Never before in her life had she trusted anyone so implicitly as she did this man. Again he gave her his quaint Eastern bow and withdrew.

It was late when she opened her eyes the following day. On attempting to move, she winced sharply. Her right leg was stiff and painful but she had slept soundly. Elfrida brought her cold meats, ale and bread and she found herself unaccountably hungry. She knew she should rise and attend to her daily tasks, but it was pleasant to lie back in the warmth and be cosseted.

When the Saracen physician called to enquire about her health, she had still not risen. He placed a cool brown hand on her forehead and smiled down at her tired countenance.

"Lady Alys," he said quietly, "you will never be well while this leg continues to pain you. You are constitutionally strong enough, but it is an effort to walk any distance and to climb the stairs. Since it appears that the joint is affected, the wet and cold weather will give you further pain."

"It is so," she nodded, "but I have learned to accommodate myself. It is only on occasions like yesterday, when I have extreme pain. There had been much to do and the weather is bad."

He sat back on the little stool by her bed, silently regarding her, and she moved nervously under his scrutiny.

"Will you allow me to examine the hip?" Elfrida rose from her seat in the shadows with a shocked gesture and he waved his hand expressively. "There can be no impropriety, with your woman present. I shall be very discreet."

Alys lay back and considered. Her father had not consulted a physician during all the years she could remember. All her life she had accepted her lameness with its associate pain. She had forced herself to do what was needed at Birlstone and early on, taken over some of her mother's more arduous tasks, when she had become ailing and frail. She had told herself that she had the stamina of other women, but knew when she glimpsed the pitying eye of an occasional visitor, that her awkwardness was an embarrassment. She raised troubled eyes to his, and he nodded gently.

"I will be very gentle and swift. I wish to know if the joint is working correctly or diseased. I may be able to help."

"Sir Geoffrey . . ."

"Sent me here to attend you."

She nodded and he turned to Elfrida, accepting at once her agreement and waiting for no further argument.

"Turn back the covers to reveal my lady's right leg. Stay by her side—so."

She felt his skilful and sensitive fingers probe the hip. He took her stiff limb and pulled it gently outwards and upwards, instructing her to press downwards and lift the limb by her own efforts. It seemed only a moment before he signed to Elfrida to re-cover her mistress and taking his seat again by her side, took her white hand in his own.

"I am relieved. The hip joint is not diseased. I am sure of it. The limb was dislocated in a fall, Sir Geoffrey said, just so. I could help you, but the treatment would take some months and would be painful. You will always limp. One leg is longer than the other but by manipulation and exercising as we Saracen physicians do, I can correct some of the trouble. Will you let me try?"

Alys swallowed and turned away. She had heard terrible stories of bone-setters who gave agony to their patients with little success. She feared further pain and worse than that, the disappointment which might follow if the treatment proved unsuccessful. He reassured her immediately.

"There will be no surgery. I shall make no incision. Early treatment will be painful and you will require courage. I have known you only a short time, but I am sure *this* you possess in plenty. The difficult part will be the long days you must stay here in bed, patiently trusting and working with me."

"But I cannot stay in my room. The manor must be inspected, work must go on . . ."

He interrupted her with a lift of his graceful hand. "The work will go on. Your bailiff is able enough. He will report to you frequently. The bad weather is upon us, when work on the manor is less demanding. This is the time—now what do you say? Choose now, for if you reject my help at once it will be harder to consider it later I know."

She smiled despite her distress. "I am a coward, Ibrahim ben Echtal. You have gauged my dastardly spirit."

"Not so, lady, if I have judged you rightly, I have naught to fear."

Alys turned to Elfrida's troubled face and then abruptly she made her decision.

"I will trust you, Ibrahim ben Echtal. Do your best for me. God knows I would wish to be an efficient wife to Sir Geoffrey and no ailing woman who cannot bear him healthy children. I have seen enough of such a marriage."

He made no comment, but rose to his feet. He left her to rest and she heard him move gracefully down the steps of the keep.

Alys would never forget that winter if she lived to be

a hundred. Afterwards she would recall with a faint shudder, the long hours of pain and weariness while she suffered under the probing fingers of the Saracen physician. He pulled and pressed, until she felt she would scream with the white hot pain, and then she would lie spent, sweat streaking down her forehead, after Elfrida had wiped down her body and attempted to make her pain-racked body more comfortable on the hard mattress. He was very gentle with her, and she rested at night under the herbal draughts he concocted for her in his little apartment off the great hall. The first few days were spent in a fever of pain and aching weariness, but gradually the suffering lessened and she was able to give attention to the affairs of the castle again.

Elfrida gossipped and told tales of the servants. Gilbert and Walter made daily reports while Elfrida presided, like a wary dragon, but it was Ibrahim himself who made the dreary weeks bearable. He had a wealth of stories for her delight, and he was a born raconteur. She was able to picture Damascus and Jerusalem, the arid desert, and she thrilled to the fears and dangers of warfare and travel in the countries she had heard so much about. The third day after her first bouts of pain had subsided, he had conveyed to her apartment the contents of three chests he had brought to Birlstone.

Both Elfrida and Alys gave cries of delight as her bed was transformed by bolt after bolt of rich shining materials, spread out for her delectation.

"This green is for you, Sir Geoffrey's first choice. The velvet he said would suit admirably the rich chestnut shade of your hair and enhance the glint in your eyes."

"He said those things, about me?" Her question was almost a whisper.

"He did indeed, how else could I have chosen so well, had he not described you accurately. See, this burgundy will make you a fine cloak, and the brocades will do later, when the weather improves."

Alys had never seen material so fine or so colourful. She touched the rich silks with timid fingers and tears came to her eyes at her husband's kindliness. She had thought him a hard man, but he had stopped his business to consider his mouselike wife away in Birlstone, and sent what he knew would most give her pleasure. Even Elfrida was quietened by the gifts and set herself to cut and stitch and embroider in a fever of creation. Some fine material in hard wearing scarlet wool had been sent for her, and the gift had left her speechless with gratitude. Alys told Ibrahim she had never known Elfrida in so happy a state before.

Sir Geoffrey wrote that he would be unable to return to Birlstone by Christmas. Ibrahim carried Alys into the great hall for the festivities. She watched with delight as the yule log was ceremonially pulled in on Christmas Eve and she was carried into the tiny chapel to hear midnight mass. As she sat with the manor serfs and men-at-arms and watched the skill of a juggler from Leicester, who had come up to the castle, seeking employment from a city desolate and on the point of starvation, she gave a little sigh, half of pleasure and half of a vague sense of disappointment. In spite of the fact that she was still confined to her couch, the Holy Season had never been so joyous at Birlstone. She was wearing a new gown of russet coloured velvet and a single chain of gold, round her hips, which held an irregular shaped chunk of deep amber, which Sir Geoffrey had sent to her from Winchester with his letter of polite regret. She had declined to wear the lovely green cotte which Elfrida had lovingly embroidered for her in gold thread. Elfrida had sulked somewhat at her refusal, as she had taken such pains to complete the garment for Christmas Day, but Alys had stood firm. She would wear it on a fitting occasion, not yet, and when she could walk in it, and with this Elfrida had to rest content. The yule log burned brightly in the fireplace and less smokily. Sir Geoffrey had gauged its shortcomings and ordered an extra trap in the roof. Her people seemed happy and content, despite the bitter iciness of the weather. They came to the manor to pay their respects and to gaze curiously at their lady in her new finery.

"Ibrahim," she said that evening after they were alone, "you read me everything Sir Geoffrey wrote?"

"Lady," his voice carried a hint of chiding, "do you think I would not?"

"You might, to spare me pain."

"Prince John keeps the Baron in Winchester. There is talk that the King had problems in the Holy Land, and John needs to discuss the news with loyal men."

"I wish that I could read for myself," she said wistfully, "the prioress of the nunnery at Rothley can do so."

"But that is easily accomplished," he laughed showing white teeth surprisingly sound against his dark bearded lip. "I will teach you. It will keep you occupied while you still are forced to rest."

"You can do this?"

"Of course."

"Sir Geoffrey writes himself?"

"Indeed yes, a clerkly hand."

"Strange," she mused, "my father could do nothing but make his mark. He swore it was no accomplishment for a knight."

Again the physician laughed. "It is a remark made by many a nobleman to cover his ineptitude. It is not so difficult. It requires perseverance and patience, neither accomplishments you lack."

In spite of Ibrahim's optimism, Alys found the art of writing more difficult than she had imagined, and it was some time before she painstakingly penned a brief note to her husband, doubtfully examining it and pursing her lips over the advisability of sending it with the Saracen's letter. He ignored her demurs and snatching it from her hand, folded and sealed the parchment and dispatched it with his own.

By the end of January, Ibrahim declared her fit to leave her bed. One cold but bright day he entered the apartment with two blocks of wood and lifted her into a sitting position on the bed. Elfrida dressed her each day now, for each evening she was carried out to eat with the household in the hall. He placed her feet gently on the blocks, then tried on her shoes of soft leather and again held her feet on the wood. She gazed at him questioningly as he took off her right shoe and examined it carefully, then he gave a bird-like nod of his head and replaced it.

"So, Lady Alys. I will take these shoes later to the shoemaker and ask him to fit a thick piece of leather on the right shoe. I think this will help solve our problem. Now stand up and take my hands. Have no fear—I will hold you tightly. That's right now, just one or two steps towards me. Steady. Do not hurry, you will feel very weak at first. Trust me and go slowly."

She could not have imagined that she would feel so faint and weak. She clung to him dizzily, while Elfrida hovered anxiously in the background, but the next day was easier and soon it was possible to walk round her small room and hesitatingly move into the hall. Only the stairs now proved an obstacle preventing her from moving freely about the castle, but Ibrahim reprovingly urged her to patience and the first buds were forming in the brushwood of the tree boles, before he watched her experimentally take the keep stairs and move out into the early sunshine of the Spring morning. From that moment, Alys knew that though it would take time, she would walk and run as other women. All her life she would limp, but no longer was she crippled. However stiff and slow her progress was, the joint was now moving freely and a thrill of elation swept through her.

It was Oswin who crouched ready to take her small foot in his hand when Walter lifted her onto the quietest palfrey in the castle stable. Strange that she felt no fear, though Ibrahim's merry eyes were clouded with anxiety, as he watched her early lessons, but Alys loved horses, though she had never mounted. She was born to ride and ride well, and by the end of the month she was able to canter through the gateway, across the drawbridge and out into the world beyond.

Chapter Four

ALYS WAS busy conferring with Father Anselm about a new altar cloth when the letter from her husband reached her. It had been a great pleasure to her to ride down to the church and herself take the measurements. The manor fields were pale green with the new shoots and the serfs waved to her as she rode by. Already the privations were being put behind them as bad dreams one thrusts into the background when the body wakes from sleep. A new Spring awaited them with new labours and new hopes and the sight of their lady on horseback, her cheeks tinged with red from the exhilaration of the ride, seemed to presage for each a triumph over hardships. Father Anselm had greeted her with tears of joy, and said prayers of gratitude on the first Sunday she attended the manor church. Now she was demanding in her choice of materials. Only the very best would do for the altar.

Ibrahim handed over the sealed missive and she looked up at him, doubtful of her ability to decipher the message. He shook his head at her lack of confidence and she broke the seal and rose to take the parchment to the slitted window to get direct light onto the carefully written letters. She could hardly believe herself capable of understanding the letter, since it gave her such delight.

"From the Baron Geoffrey de Courcelles to my Lady Alys, greetings.

"I have now returned from my castle on the Welsh border and have taken a town house in Castlegate, Nottingham, where I am now in attendance on the Prince, who is here for the fair and jousting which begin next week. Since Ibrahim ben Echtal tells me you are well enough to travel, I request you join me here, and enjoy the spectacle of the tournament. The town is pleasant enough in this season and a change of scene should interest you."

Ibrahim scanned the letter and returned it. "The change will be beneficial. You will be able to meet many of your husband's friends. You are too secluded here. I have thought it since I arrived."

"He means it? I am to go? Ibrahim, I have only left Birlstone once in my life. Four years ago I spent three days in Nottingham when I purchased new materials with my father. I was fascinated with the town, but he never took me again and I am to see the festivities—truly?"

"It seems so. Gilbert can be trusted. I will travel with you."

"I may ride?"

He pursed his lips. "We will take a litter. You are new to the saddle and it is no short journey for you, part of the way perhaps, but do not overtire yourself too soon."

"Father Anselm, I will purchase more gold and silver thread. It is just what I need for the design of the altar cloth. I was expecting to wait for the annual visit of the pedlar and he often has nothing so fine, now I can really do what I wish."

The priest rose smiling. "My child, I am delighted for your sake that the work will be delayed. As you say, it will be finer than ever, when completed."

Three feverish days were spent in preparation. Even Elfrida became irritable at her mistress's repeated changes in decisions. First one garment, then the other, was discarded, but at last the travelling chests were packed and Gilbert given his instructions. He was courteous enough, though somewhat surly and Ibrahim frowned a little at his tone, though Alys was too excited to note it. She looked ruefully at the litter which the physician had ordered to accompany them, but made no comment. Walter assisted her into the saddle of her grey palfrey and the little troop mounted and prepared to leave.

It was a cold sunny April morning but Alys, wrapped warmly in her new cloak of russet velvet lined with fur, saw only its golden freshness. Elfrida exclaimed over her eagerness to forge ahead, fearing the ride through the manor and onwards through Mountsorrel and past the nunnery at Rothley, would be too much for her mistress. Ibrahim was content. He had arranged that they should rest at a small inn on the way and there he would insist that she lie down for a while, and the litter was ready, should she tire. He rode slightly behind her, smiling at her obviously youthful delight in her surroundings. The road was hard, since the night had been dry and frosty, and the going was easy enough. The horses trotted at a good pace and the men-at-arms, conscious that they needed no attention to pick their way, tended to gossip and ride without undue notice to their journey. Once past Rothley, they met a few travellers and at last the road entered a shaded portion, bordered on either side by tall oaks. Once or twice a deer, startled by the sound of their horses' hoofs and upraised voices, darted across the road ahead of them, and rustlings in the hedgerows betrayed the presence of smaller living creatures. Alys shaded her eyes as she looked upwards at a squirrel, who scrambled skywards into an elm. She called Ibrahim's attention to the little creature and he drew reign to follow her gaze. Their attention taken as it was they failed to notice the small group of men ahead of them, and it was a muttered imprecation from Walter, which warned them of the approach of the newcomers. Startled, Alys turned from the elm tree, sanctuary of her squirrel friend, to find that the way was barred by a troop of twenty men, who levelled drawn bows to show they meant business.

"Walter, what is the meaning of this?" Alarmed as she was, Alys's voice was clear and did not falter as she gestured imperiously for her captain-at-arms to join her.

His narrowed eyes took in the silent line of men. "An ambush, Lady Alys. These men are wolf's heads—outlaws. They live on what they can kill and steal from passers-by."

"Your man-at-arms explains the situation admirably, lady," a quiet voice broke across his explanation. "As he said, we need to take the purses of travellers to survive." He shrugged, "We cannot exist on game alone and the foresters press us hardly."

Alys regarded the outlaw leader coldly. He appeared no desperate ruffian, a man of middle age, grizzled at the temples, dressed in a rough homespun tunic of russet coloured woollen material and down at heel leathern boots, fashioned of animal skins and roughly sewn.

"I see no reason why you needed to leave your village," she said icily. "No excuse can be strong enough to prey upon unsuspecting travellers as we are. Nevertheless, since I am determined to avoid bloodshed, you may take what you will. I have little enough to give."

"You would find it hard to understand my reasons, lady." He bowed slightly and she noted with surprise that his voice was pleasant, even cultured, not that of a serf. "Let us say I have no time to proffer them, they are many and varied. You will perhaps be Lady Alys FitzAlan of Birlstone."

"I am the wife of Baron Geoffrey de Courcelles, who will doubtless seek you out and punish you for this outrage," she said angrily jerking her palfrey to a halt, as it sidled nervously forward. She was irritated by the sudden interruption of her pleasant interlude and was in no mood for polite exchanges, especially from an outlaw.

"So," he gave a wry twist to his mouth, "the Prince married you to a friend. That was clever of him. From what I have heard of the Baron, he may well do what you say. You may proceed, lady, I have no quarrel with you."

"Walter, give these thieves what they demand. There is to be no brawling."

The captain looked behind to his men and then gazed for further assurance at the Saracen, who had remained silent until now.

"Take no risks, captain, not while Lady Alys rides with us. We are too few in numbers and these men were prepared." His voice dropped a tone, "There will be other occasions."

The captain grunted his assent and called an order to two of the men who guarded one of the baggage mules.

"You mistake me, Lady Alys," the outlaw said quietly. "I said you may proceed. News comes to me here and I know your serfs fare well enough at Birlstone. We will take from less deserving wayfarers."

"A gallant cut-throat," her scorn was directed full at him. "I find it no compliment, sir, to be treated discriminately by a beggarly Saxon, an outlaw to boot."

He was not angered but held up both arms high in the air. At this signal, the men ahead lowered their bows from their threatening positions and drew aside to allow the small band to pass. Lady Alys swept by their leader, who again bowed to her, a trifle mockingly.

Ibrahim allowed himself a little sigh of relief. He had feared that Lady Alys's contempt might fan some flame of resentment in the little band of outlaws, and he feared the outcome of a skirmish. She had yet little skill in riding and was already appearing a little strained and wan. The encounter had alarmed her, although she gave no sign. He considered it strange that the thief had not demanded gold from them, but was content to continue the journey and hope there would be no further disturbing incidents, which might threaten the safety of his erstwhile patient. He spurred ahead to join her.

It was then that he heard the sound of pursuit and

an armed band of men rode into the clearing. They were well mounted, armed and wore mail, obviously trained fighting men. The outlaw chief called to his men who hastily drew back into the woods behind. One dropped to his knees and drew his bow but the forward man rode him down and he fell screaming under the horse's hoofs. Before he could retreat after his men, the leader was surrounded. A sturdy archer dismounted and knocked him to his knees. Alys turned to see the prisoner securely bound and hobbled in a few moments and turned back with a sharp cry of pity as again he received a heavy blow on the side of his head from the hilt of a two handed sword wielded by another of the mailed men.

"Do not disturb yourself, lady, as to the fate of such scum," a slightly drawled musical voice arrested her attention. "He is not worth your concern."

She looked back at the speaker who had ridden up to join his men. He rode completely unarmed and without mail, a slight graceful figure on a coal black charger, leaning back easily in the saddle to set off to perfection his long tunic of purple silk and cloak of black velvet, with its lilac coloured lining. His black velvet cap was set at a rakish angle and he was quite the most handsome man Alys had ever seen. Auburn hair fell to his shoulders and his small pointed beard was groomed to perfection. Grey sleepy eyes regarded her smilingly over a straight, aquiline nose and thin well-shaped lips. Ibrahim noted that there was no warmth in the smile, though the man was anxious to put his young fellow traveller at her ease.

"For some months I have been anxious to talk to this fellow. It seems you have done me a service, lady, since in robbing you, he gave me the opportunity to catch up with him. On various other occasions, he has slipped through my fingers."

"You know this man?" she sounded surprised, not altogether relieved.

"Indeed yes," the elegant young knight smiled wolf-

ishly at his prisoner, "we know each other very well.
Do we not, Rolf?"

The man did not answer and Alys noticed that his
lower lip was swollen from a blow dealt by one of his
captors.

"Do not think of him again. He is a run-away serf. I
will deal with him at my own court, but he must await
my return. I am on my way to Nottingham. Permit me
to introduce myself, William de Lacey, keeper of
Mountsorrel for Robert FitzParnel, Earl of Leicester."

"You are addressing the Lady Alys, wife of Baron
Geoffrey de Courcelles."

Ibrahim briefly affected the introduction and did not
fail to note the man's insolent stare at his foreign attire,
though he passed no comment.

"Well met indeed, lady. I have many times heard of
my neighbour, but had not expected to find her so
beautiful."

Alys blushed hotly at his affected gallantry. Already
the outlaw leader had been hustled away and though
pity vied within her with an admiration for his handsome young captor, she knew nothing could be done
for the man at this stage, and she smiled graciously at
Sir William.

"You find us on our way to Nottingham, Sir
William," she said, "I am grateful for your arrival, although in fact, the man had taken nothing from us,
and said that he wished us well."

"Indeed," Sir William smiled lazily. "The devil
grows kind. He is not so old, lady, that like me he has
fallen under the spell of your beauty. However I cannot allow you to proceed without escort, in case further
attacks interfere with your comfort. May I offer myself
as protector and accompany you? If you accept, it will
give me the greatest pleasure."

"You are kind, Sir," Alys's tone was warm. "I would
be grateful but doubtless you could proceed more
quickly if not burdened by such a responsibility. I have
been ill. I can ride but slowly."

Again Sir William smiled, "Lady, the added length of the journey fills me with even greater delight."

"You talk nonsense, Sir Knight," Alys said but her tone was not sharp and the knight rode to her side, accepting her words as compliance. Six of the men-at-arms took the lead and the rest brought up the rear, four of them having ridden back to Mountsorrel with the prisoner. Ibrahim drew back to ride with Walter. One glance at the weathered face of the captain-at-arms confirmed his own belief that he was not altogether pleased by their neighbour's arrival on the scene.

Despite her alarm at the unprecedented attack, Alys did not find the second phase of her journey unpleasant. The novelty of Sir William's company proved a welcome diversion, and she had not realised quite how tired she was until they dismounted at an ale house in Bunney. Sir William called imperiously for a private screened bench, as the hostelry was too poor to provide a separate room, graciously invited Ibrahim to accompany them, and conveyed Alys to the wooden settle near the fire. Ibrahim nodded his acceptance, but first moved outside to speak with Walter and arrange for the use of the litter, should it be required after the meal. It was therefore several minutes before he joined them.

Alys put back her hood and loosened her furred mantle. Sir William smiled at her childish gesture in holding her hands to the blaze. If he had noted her awkard gait on leading her into the inn, he made no reference to it. She had found him an engaging companion as he talked of the Prince and of the King whom he had seen once or twice only, of Longchamps, de Burgh, and many other nobles, whose names only had been known to her. Snippets of gossip he imparted brought a smile to her lips, and though jocular, he was never actually salacious. She had looked forward to her stay in Nottingham. Now she felt she knew more about what would be expected of her.

Now as she leaned forward to the fire, her girdle of

gold and amber, Sir Geoffrey's Christmas gift, unexpectedly fell to the ground with a clatter. Sir William bent forward to retrieve it and examined the amber curiously.

"This is very strange and fine. I have never seen anything like it."

"Ibrahim tells me it is amber. The pieces of it came from the shores of the Northern Sea. Its yellow colour is very lovely."

"It is indeed. I have heard of the substance, but never seen it. The texture is smooth and pleasing to the touch. I see the clasp is broken."

"Oh is it?" she reached for the girdle, consternation apparent on her young face, "that is unfortunate. It is a new gift from my husband. I wished to show him that I wear it constantly."

"Allow me to have it repaired for you, lady. I know a Jewish goldsmith in the town. He is a skilled worker. He will attend to the matter speedily."

Alys was confused. "But, Sir William, I cannot ask you to take such trouble."

"Lady, you overstate the issue. This is no trouble. I know the town and its craftsmen. You do not. Allow me the pleasure of dealing with this for you."

"If you insist, Sir. You are very kind," she faltered as Ibrahim came up to join them.

Sir William swept the costly chain into the large finely studded purse which was suspended from his belt and rose to call the attention of the landlord to their needs. Ibrahim was pleased to note that Alys seemed none the worse for her experiences. She was youthfully eager to impart to him some of the information gained, and he smiled at her pleasure. After a frugal but satisfying meal, they resumed their journey, and in spite of Ibrahim's urging, Alys was adamant in her refusal to continue in the litter, so he was forced to give way, and so it was that Alys entered Nottingham, riding, as she had wished. Sir Geoffrey himself lifted her from the saddle on her arrival at the small house in Castlegate, and carried her affectionately inside.

Chapter Five

ALYS STARED like a wonder-struck child at the sight of unprecedented splendour before her as she sat in the pavilion with other exalted guests, her eyes roaming everywhere in an attempt to miss nothing. For the moment, the green sward of the lists lay empty for the tourney had not yet begun. At each end of the open grass space, banners flew on poles round the two pavilions where the knights who were to take part, were being armed by their squires. On the opposite side of the lists, thronged the townsfolk of Nottingham, voluble and in holiday mood, sweating, quarrelling, eating noisily and laying bets on the opponents.

"The sight pleases you, Lady Alys?" the courteous question caused her to blush nervously, as she turned towards the speaker.

She would never get used to the presence of the Prince. He had placed her on his left, a seat of honour, and had engaged her in polite conversation since her husband had presented her. He made a splendid figure in cloth of gold, his gold Plantagenet hair falling onto his shoulders in a heavy cloud. He was handsome enough, with straight regular features, fine green flecked eyes, which she imagined could blaze in sudden rage if the mood took him, and only a hint of petulant discontent marred the pleasing features. So this was John Lackland the Prince without an inheritance, whom people were already quietly accusing of plotting against his brother and secretly attempting to arrange that he would not return home. Alys had found herself unable to stare but also caught herself thinking that

44

perhaps the man was misjudged. Cruel and sensual he might be, but he was no fool. Sir Geoffrey had forbore to comment, but she guessed that he held a steady respect for this man, who had been left to manage the unruly knights and barons who had not chosen to accompany the Lion Heart to the Holy Land. England writhed under a heavy burden of taxation, for Richard had bled her white to provide the equipment and pay the fighting men he needed for the Holy War. It was no wonder that the people seethed with discontent and murmured against the lords, and for this reason it had been deemed wiser to keep the curfew law which the conquerer had earlier imposed, so that his unwilling Saxon subjects would find it nigh impossible to gather together unlawfully for secret discussions after the hours of darkness. The townsfolk certainly showed no animosity towards their Prince on this bright sunny April day, and Alys herself had no fault to find with his kind reception of her.

"Indeed, Sire, I cannot believe that I am really here. It is the first time for me."

"It does not bring unhappy thoughts?"

She flushed darkly and lowered her head at memories of her father's mishap on this same spot, only last year.

"My father loved the joust, Sire. It was the way he would have wished to die."

"True—the man was fearless. He took much gold and ransom during the occasions on which he took part. We are delighted that the Baron thought fit to bring you. He has spoken much of you, and indeed I find he did not overestimate your beauty. You have the pleasing freshness of the true English woman, and I am gratified to find you recovered. I had heard you were ill."

"My new Saracen physician has performed a miracle, Sire. I still limp it is true, but I can now ride and move freely enough. Sir Geoffrey himself is pleased to note my progress."

The prince nodded smiling. "I hope soon to hear

that you have provided an heir to succeed in holding Birlstone loyally for the crown."

"You are kind, Sire." Alys felt her complexion darken again and lowered her eyes. She was relieved when the Prince turned his attention to a churchman on his right and stared once more over the lists. Sir Geoffrey had not thought to joust, but had agreed to take part in the mêlée, which was to end the day's sport, and the seat beside her was empty, as he had entered the pavilion nearest to her, to arm with his Squire Alain Guilbert.

She had spent a pleasant week in the little house in Castlegate. Despite its smallness, it was well appointed and they had private apartments in which the tapestries and furnishings had appeared amazingly luxurious to Alys, who had rarely strayed from the military comfortless security of Birlstone Castle. He had been delighted to see her new facility of movement but had insisted on complete rest. He continued to treat her with the polite restraint one used towards a stranger, but had not spared expense or trouble to attend to her comfort. It was for him that she had dressed today in the soft green velvet gown with its gold embroidered bands and had donned her best wimple of finest lawn. Sir William had not returned the girdle of amber, so she wore a soft leather belt of darker green encircling her hips, studded with gold and embellished with matching gold thread of the gown itself. One glance of approval Sir Geoffrey had given her, before presenting her to Prince John, and she knew she had surprised him with the elegance of her apparel.

Now he came to her side, mailed and ready for combat. She smiled up at him and at his Squire Alain who held his helmet and took his place behind him. The trumpets sounded and the first two contestants rode into the lists and drew rein before the royal pavilion. The crowd roared its approval that the entertainment was now beginning. The two young knights bowed from the saddle at their prince and inclined their plumed helmets toward Alys, whom the Prince had graciously declared Queen of the Tournament. She waved smiling, as she saw one young man gaze towards a pretty dark girl who sat with her elderly father, some feet away. Alys knew that the blue glove which dangled from his helmet was her favour, and for her he hoped to unseat his opponent today. The Prince lifted high in the air an ornamental gold baton and the two rode to their places at opposite ends of the lists.

A sudden hush fell on the crowd, and the people leaned forward expectantly. Alys told herself there should be no danger. The antagonists fought with blunted lances and merely attempted to thrust their opponent from the saddle. The church had frowned on the tournament, declaring it blood lust, for many fine young knights had met their deaths in the lists, but it was a favourite sport with the English and King Richard had defied the ban and allowed jousting to continue within limits and in certified places. Well enough, he knew he must keep the favour of his subjects if they were to willingly loose their purse strings for him to continue his wars in the Holy Land. Alys's pulse beat faster as she followed the younger knight with her eyes. He had lowered his visor but she saw his lady's favour bravely blow in the faint breeze and hoped he would acquit himself well in her eyes. The horses pounded forward. Alys felt her husband lean towards his squire to comment on the chances of one or other of the combatants. Dull thuds sounded as both shields were struck squarely, but both rode on to the other end of the lists, neither was unhorsed. Grooms sprang forward to take the chargers' bridles, and to hand up fresh lances, since the used ones, were now splintered. She noted the pear shaped foils as once more the two wheeled their mounts for the second charge. Again a flurry of raised dust, thunder of horses' hoofs and a shout of triumph as the older man fell from his saddle to lie still in the dust. For one moment Alys prayed softly. Her own father had fallen thus, and had never risen again but no, all was well, the man was up and moving slowly to his pavilion. Now his accoutre-

ments and horse would be the property of the victor.
She hoped that it might be possible for the young man
to woo and win his lady.

As bout after bout followed with no damage to man
or horse, Alys relaxed her anxious excitement and sat
back to enjoy the spectacle. The Prince leaned towards
her to explain features of the contests, and Sir Geoffrey
smiled gravely at her enjoyment. It was one contestant
in the fourth joust who seized her attention, and made
her catch her breath suddenly and sharply. He was
clad from head to foot in black chain mail. Even his
surcoat was of sable, lightened only by a white shield
bearing a mailed glove. But it was not the sombre, yet
elegant appearance of the knight, which startled Alys
but the sight of a chain of gold, which he wore round
his neck, from which hung an irregular piece of amber.
The knight rode to his place before the pavilion, raised
his visor and bowed towards the Prince. She had a
glimpse of white gleaming teeth as he smiled in her
direction and raised one hand in salute, then he wheeled
his charger to take his place in the lists. Alys was horror
stricken, she hardly dared to face her husband and
took no note of the joust. Sir Geoffrey seemed completely unmoved, but there was a steely glitter in his
light eyes which alarmed her. As she made to speak,
to blurt out some explanation, he raised one eyebrow
in polite interrogation, then ignoring her, turned back
to the contest.

De Lacey had easily unhorsed his opponent and
was now dismounting to re-enter his pavilion. Fran-
tically Alys thought what she must say, but her husband was rising. He was making his excuses to the
Prince who nodded smiling. He was to ride in the
mêlée against the troop of victorious knights. The
Prince appeared not to notice Alys's alarm and explained that the mêlée was a mock combat entered
into by five knights on each side. The man who best
acquitted himself would receive a small wreath of
golden laurel leaves which she, as Queen of the Tournament, would present. It was likely to be de Lacey, he

said, the man was one of the more experienced knights and had unhorsed his antagonist in the first bout. It was true there was some danger in the confusion of the mêlée but Sir Geoffrey was safe enough. He had ridden in too many to be in danger. He knew how to withstand the shock of impact when lance thudded on shield and he was an accomplished rider, unlikely to be thrown from the saddle under the unfuriated hoofs of the war maddened chargers.

As the trumpets sounded the attack, the ten knights thundered into the lists. Alys could pick out the golden gryphon on Sir Geoffrey's white surcoat, and also the dull gleam of golden amber on the sable one of de Lacey's. How could he have so humiliated her? Innocent of court intrigues and gossip as she was, Alys knew well enough that the wearing of a favour of another man's wife was a deadly insult, and she feared her husband's anger, both for de Lacey, whom he was now facing in mock combat, and for herself, for a reckoning would be demanded of her when this was over. She cursed her folly in not telling him of her encounter with the neighbouring knight, nor of his promise to have the amber girdle repaired. It had slipped her memory in the thrill of greeting, and examining the small house in Castlegate; the joy of new sights and sounds, of the pleasure of shopping for silk thread and materials of ribbons and gifts for some of the household. She had simply not given one thought to her journey. Her life had been taken up with talk of new experiences and the delight of ease in walking, which until now had been denied her. She knew now that Sir Geoffrey would consider her reticence about her acquaintance with de Lacey, to be suspicious in the extreme.

The crowd called out encouragement to the combatants. Horses neighed in shrill accents as the two opposing sides rode towards each other. Dust rose in swirls as horses and men were locked in deadly combat. Sport it might be, but dangerous to life and limb. Already two knights were down and a small knot of grooms attempted to drag them to safety out of reach of the hoofs of their terrified mounts. She lowered her head for a moment from the terrifying sight of men lost for a few moments to decency, filled with lust of combat. She could distinguish nothing for a while when she lifted her head, then abruptly, three more men were down and she saw her husband's white surcoat with its golden gryphon crest, clearly. He had thrown down his splintered lance and was fighting with an intense savagery with broadsword. Again and again she saw him sweep the heavy weapon at the black robed chest of his opponent. Soon the crowd was hushed to watch these two alone fight out the completion of the event. They were well matched. De Lacey rode like a centaur and parried the other's blows with ease, then some slight sound from the pavilion disturbed him and claimed his attention. For one second he half turned and with a savage blow Sir Geoffrey took the advantage and knocked him from the saddle. A roar from the crowd acknowledged his victory, but surprisingly, he did not ride off while the other staggered to his feet, but kicked his own mail shod shoes free from the stirrups and sprang to the ground.

The Prince gave a half smothered oath as Sir Geoffrey stood still while his opponent rose slowly, half bemused by the fall. De Lacey had lost his sword and Sir Geoffrey threw down his own. Alys heard the dull clang as it dropped in the dust, then he stood back and drew his dagger. De Lacey shook his head to clear the mist, then slowly put his hand to his own weapon. The steward of the tournament anxiously pushed his way through the spectators in the pavilion and whispered urgently to the Prince.

"Highness, the rules of the tournament are being disobeyed. Will you declare the bout at an end?"

"Leave them for a while. We will watch closely."

The man drew back, but his heavy breathing showed his continued alarm. Alys gripped the carved arms of her gilded chair, tightly. Her husband was pressing the man to a fight to the finish and she knew why. If harm came to either, it would be her fault, yet she knew she was innocent of wrongful intent. She sent up a prayer to the Virgin for aid. Even should Sir Geoffrey wound or slay his opponent and come unscathed himself from the fight, he would be forced to stand trial, since the rules of this tournament had been fashioned to prevent injury to man or mount.

The two men were circling warily. It was clear that de Lacey had been startled by the turn events had taken. Perhaps he had only determined to tease his neighbour and been unaware of the fact that he was to take part in the mêlée. Skilled fighter that he was, it was clear that he was uncertain of himself. Twice he stumbled and almost fell, and the crowd expelled its breath with a little sigh which sounded over the whole length of the lists, then he gave a gurgling cry, almost muffled by his mailed helmet and fell backwards. Sir Geoffrey leaned over his prostrate form and pressed his dagger point against the weakest part where helmet and mail parted and the pulse of the throat could be seen by the startled grooms who waited nearby to try to avert tragedy. Deeper he pressed and the crowd was silenced, then abruptly he rose and stood back. De Lacey lay still as if afraid to move, then slowly drew himself to his feet. Then and then only did the crowd roar its approval.

Alys thrust her linen handkerchief in a tight ball against her ashen lips and sank back in her chair. It was over, neither man had been injured, but she knew well enough, how close it had been.

The Prince rose to his feet, eager to close the proceedings and cover any ill feelings which might still exist. The crowd must now disperse without a bitter taste of ill will in its mouth and he announced the name of the champion. The tournament steward placed the ornamental wreath into Alys's cold little hands, and she rose mechanically and placed it on the lowered lance of the young knight of the glove, repeating some polite words of congratulation, which she knew were expected of her. Her husband had not yet reappeared from his pavilion, and she allowed herself to be drawn away by the Prince to feast with his friends in the Great Hall of the castle.

Ibrahim and Roul escorted her to the house in Castlegate. She stayed within her own room with Elfrida, until some hours later, she was summoned to the Hall. Sir Geoffrey sat at the oaken table completing some writing. He rose when she entered, and motioned her to seat herself opposite. She complied at once, and nervously considered what she would say when he questioned her.

"I am sending you early tomorrow back to Birlstone," he said coldly. "This time you will be escorted by Captain Roul. Walter may stay here to serve me. I shall be a few more days in Nottingham in attendance on the Prince. Until that time, I insist that you stay within the precincts of the castle. Roul will have my instructions. Please do not make life difficult for him by questioning his authority."

Her face flushed scarlet. "You intend to keep me a prisoner."

"I think I have made my wishes clear."

"Sir Geoffrey, I insist that you listen. You cannot treat me like a refractory child. What have I done wrong?"

His brow contracted in a frown and his tone was icy, "I hardly think we need discuss that matter, Madam."

"Of what are you accusing me? I met Sir William de Lacey on the way to Nottingham. He . . ."

"Indeed, this is the first I have heard about your meeting."

"There was no time. We have been busy—I was so excited by the town, please you must understand . . ." Alys rose, anxious to explain, but his coldness had both confused and angered her.

"All I know, Madam, is that de Lacey wore your favour in the lists. A favour indeed—which was my first gift."

"I did not give him the girdle . . ."

"Please, Madam, do not trouble yourself to give excuses. The matter is over. I trust no harm has been done. You will not see de Lacey again. Roul will accompany you in the morning. When I return, I will further consider the matter."

"I do not understand—what is there to consider?"

"The matter of your punishment, Madam."

"My punishment?" Alys sprang up again, this time fury sharpening her voice. "How dare you, Sir Geoffrey. You insult me, accuse me of impossible crimes, then dare to speak of chastisement. I am no silly chit to take lying down, what treatment you choose to give me. I am mistress of Birlstone. You will soon discover that my servants still look to me for their orders. I do not intend to remain and argue with you. You must be mad to think such things. I have done nothing deserving your reproaches, let alone your discipline." Tears threatened, and determined that he should not see her cry, she turned and made blindly for the door but she was still clumsy on her feet, and half blinded with rage, stumbled against a small carved stool which she had not noticed. She fell heavily, and for a moment was unable to rise. Immediately he was at her side and leaned down to lift her to her feet. She angrily pushed him away, but he persisted and lifting her up, placed her on the chair again.

"Leave me alone. I am not hurt. Let me go."

"Rest for a moment. You are winded," he turned as Elfrida hurried into the hall and stopped short at the overturned stool and the sight of her mistress, near enough to tears.

"Your mistress stumbled. I think she will be well enough in a few moments. I am glad you are here, Elfrida. I was about to send for you."

"My Lord?"

"Elfrida, I have requested that Lady Alys does not leave Birlstone, not even to go into the village. You understand?"

"Yes—but my lord . . ."

"Do not interrupt me, Elfrida." He paused and the Saxon woman looked up startled at the icy glitter of those blue eyes. "I will be explicit, Elfrida. If I find you have disobeyed me and left Birlstone with your mistress, even at her request, you will leave the castle within the hour and never return. I make myself clear?"

Elfrida's face went white and she curtseyed low. "Yes, my lord," she whispered.

"Good. Assist my wife to her room. Summon Ibrahim if she needs help. It is unlikely that I shall see you again before I join you at Birlstone at the end of the week, but mark my words."

He turned without another word and left the room. Elfrida slipped to her knees before her mistress's chair. She was shocked to see that Alys's face was pale and set. Her knuckles gleamed white as she clutched tightly at the arms of her chair. There were no tears. Already Alys had recovered herself. She rose.

"Come, Elfrida," she said through stiffened lips, "you heard your master well enough. Come with me to my room. There is nothing further to be said. We have been given our orders."

✌ Chapter Six

ALYS STARED down at the unfinished altar cloth she had begun with such a joyful heart. It no longer claimed her attention. The bright threads she had chosen in Nottingham with such care now seemed garish and without taste. Elfrida, seated opposite, sensed her restlessness but said nothing. She cut her own thread and sought to distract her mistress from the thought uppermost in her mind. Elfrida was frightened. She had seen Alys in all moods from deep despondency to enthusiastic delight, but never before had she glimpsed what was now in her heart. The girl had always been sensible, patient with her ailing mother and unfailingly obedient to her blustering father, but today there was a mutinous twist to the lips which had not been there before. Alys was angry, coldly furious and Elfrida feared that she meant to rebel. Her heart stirred with fear. She dare not involve herself in her mistress's disobedience though she longed to say something which would comfort her, she knew any words she might utter would only fan the flames of open revolt.

Viciously Alys stabbed at the white silk. How dare he treat her like a child in her own castle; refuse to listen to explanations. She had never felt such a fool. Yesterday she had been forced to ask Father Anselm to trudge once more up to the castle instead of herself attending the manor church. He had asked no questions but she had sensed his curiosity. She had been too proud to tell him what had happened, or had she feared that he too might misunderstand? That first night in Castlegate, she had sobbed into her pillow. All the happiness which the unexpected visit had given her had evaporated suddenly in a cloud of anger and distrust. She had determined to say no further words to him. If he believed her guilty of deliberately impugning his honour, then she would allow him to do so. She would not stoop to beg him to listen. He had not been present when the little cavalcade had left Nottingham, and she had ridden silently by Elfrida's side, with an embarrassed Roul behind her. Although she was almost exhausted by the lengthy ride, she refused to ask the captain-at-arms to stop and rest, and they had reached Birlstone well before nightfall. Sir Geoffrey was not expected back until the end of the week, and she refused to think of his threatened chastisement. He would not dare.

Her thoughts turned to de Lacey. His conduct remained inexplicable. Why had he done such a foolish and seemingly cruel act? She had given him no cause

to think she found him attractive. Her head jerked up
abruptly and she put down the embroidery and rose to
her feet.

"It is too fine a morning to remain indoors, Elfrida,
I'll visit the stables."

"My Lady," the maid eyed her anxiously, "you will
not venture beyond the gate?"

"I am hardly likely to be allowed to," Alys snapped,
"Roul watches me like a hawk. It is intolerable."

"Sir Geoffrey will soon return, lady."

"That fact hardly brings me pleasure. Nay—stay
here, Elfrida, you hate to dirty your shoes you know. I
will not be long." She ran lightly down the stairs,
hardly remembering her painful descent of a few
months ago. Her limp was now only apparent when
she was tired, and it was frustrating, now that she
could ride out to inspect the work of the manor, to be
prevented from doing so. She avoided Roul, who was
crossing the bailey. His quiet respect irked her, for she
knew he hated the necessity to keep her a prisoner, but
dared not disobey his master's orders. She entered the
gloom of the stable and paused to pat her palfrey's
questing nose. She was surprised to find Oswin within.

"I am sorry if I startled you, lady. I called to see
Jehan about some lotion. Hella has strained a muscle.
He promised to make some up for me."

"She is badly hurt?"

"No, lady, but she is limping."

"I am sorry. She must rest for a while."

"That is the difficulty, lady. Hella is used to her
freedom. She whines when she sees me leave the hut.
She wants to feel the cool air, and grass under the
feet."

Alys sighed and turned from him. "I can feel for
her."

He was silent and she turned back to him. When she
spoke her tone was bitter.

"So even you know I am a prisoner in my own
house."

He was embarrassed. "It has been whispered, lady."

"It is infuriating. A situation I will not tolerate. Oswin, I refuse to stay cooped here. I wish to ride—and ride I will, but how can I get out through the gate?"

Oswin's reply was cautious. "It is not difficult to get through the gate, lady, but to ride out is a different matter."

"You mean on foot, it could be managed?" Immediately, she was all eagerness.

"The guards are not concerned about the village girls who come and go when they wish. My sister often comes to the castle to help in the kitchen."

"And passes out through the gate. Oswin, I see your point. Can you arrange for her to come to my apartment to help with some mending?"

"That is easily accomplished, lady."

"I could wear her dress and walk out."

"Easily. If you wish to ride I could manage the rest. Lady, can you walk to the village?"

"Yes, I'm sure I can."

"There is a little copse behind the inn, near the river. Do you know it?"

She nodded. "I will find it."

"There I will await you with your horse. It is simple."

Alys was delighted. For the sheer pleasure of outwitting Sir Geoffrey, she was determined to leave the castle, but her face clouded as she thought of the boy's part in the affair.

"Oswin, if Sir Geoffrey knows you have helped me, he will be angry."

The boy laughed merrily. "Lady," he chaffed her gently, "it is born in a serf to know how to outwit his Lord, truly, I should not reveal such a secret."

"You will be careful?"

"Yes, lady, I swear it for your sake as well as my own."

Alys found it difficult to conceal her mounting impatience as she moved about the keep. Elfrida was puzzled by her change in mood, and talked current village gossip. Sir William de Lacey had returned to

Mountsorrel. There had been trouble in Nottingham with another knight, some said. The man was born to cause trouble. Local countryfolk hoped it would keep the marauding knight safe in his own territory, if only for a while. So de Lacey was home. Alys had been furious at his treatment of her. He had not returned her girdle, or if he had surrendered it to Sir Geoffrey, he had told her nothing. Suppose she was to pay him a surprise visit. He might be persuaded to explain his conduct, and at the same time the act of deliberate disobedience to her husband's command added piquancy to the afternoon's adventure. She smiled a little but said nothing.

Elfrida was surprised when Oswin's sister arrived at the keep and announced that the Lady Alys had sent for her to help with some mending of linen. She was about to expostulate when Alys moved her firmly aside and led the girl into her apartment. Marian was a rosy cheeked impudent little creature, several years younger than her lady but fortunately they were much about the same height. She placed a largish bundle on the floor and giggled.

"My Lady will not wish to wear my clothes on her ride. She may carry her own in the bundle, and I have brought my others to change. See, I have put on my best, indeed, lady, I have only the two kirtles you see, but this one is clean enough."

Horrified, Elfrida watched the young serf step from her russet kirtle of homespun and stand in her shift before them both. From the bundle, she extracted her working dress, stained and patched and slipped it on.

"My Lady," Elfrida said shocked, as she stooped and picked up the discarded garment, "you are not planning to leave Birlstone, not in this?"

"I am, Elfrida," Alys hastily drew off her own garments and held out her hand impatiently to take the kirtle, "now don't fret I shall be safe enough and back before sundown."

"But Sir Geoffrey . . ."

"Will know nothing about it. I know, Elfrida, you

are disturbed by his threat. All you have to do is to keep Marian here in my apartment, until I return. She will help you with the sewing. Later, we will send her home with gifts."

Alys let down her brown hair from the caul under the wimple and donned a simple brown kerchief to cover it. If the guard did not look too closely, she would pass well enough, and why should he? She indicated to Elfrida which dress she would take and her nurse, shaking her head and muttering words of disapproval, packed the bundle again and held it out to her.

"Watch your step on the road."

"I will walk slowly. If anyone questions me, I shall say I sprained my foot."

"If anyone questions you," Elfrida retorted dourly, "they will know at once you are no serf. Lady Alys, what has put such a fool notion into your head, to act so rashly? You never before behaved so."

"No," Alys paused in the doorway, "no, I did not. Perhaps it is because I can walk now as other maids or . . ." she paused then laughed a trifle bitterly, "or perhaps it is because I am no longer a maid, I have a husband who guards me well."

It proved a simple matter after all to leave the castle. Captain Roul was busy on the battlements and the man-at-arms on guard duty at the portcullis was more than half asleep in the warm sun. He contented himself with a good-humoured bawdy comment as she passed him and she was out on the road. On horseback it had seemed no distance to the village but the dirt road was dusty and the stones hurt her feet. The bundle was an unaccustomed weight and she was glad when she saw the first dirt cottages along the way, and the tower of the church. It was easy to identify the inn The White Horse, and behind it on the bank of the Soar, was the small copse of elm and birch trees. Oswin stood well back in the shade, and in his care were two horses, her own grey palfrey and a small sturdy welsh pony, which Sir Geoffrey had brought with him to Birlstone. He smiled when he saw her, and indicated a convenient brake where she might change. When she returned to his side, she was laughing a little as she thrust two thick braids of brown hair well under the hood of her riding cloak. Without Elfrida's assistance it had not been easy to deal with it.

"Thank you, Oswin. You have done well. How did you manage to lead out the palfrey?"

"Simple, lady, she cast a nail. I brought her to the Smithy."

"I see. Now back with you to Birlstone." He shook his head decisively.

"No, lady, I go with you. You cannot ride alone."

"Oswin, I won't allow it. You are already involved. Sir Geoffrey would punish you harshly if he knew your part in this affair. To progress further would be doubly dangerous."

The boy made no comment. He mounted and waited, and shaking her head sadly, she urged her mount forward and noted thankfully that he was following, as she took the road towards Mountsorrel.

Had she thought seriously about what she intended, she knew she would have never proceeded, but the afternoon was so glorious. It seemed so wonderful to be away from the castle and her husband's retainers, who reminded her of her humiliation. Angry colour flooded her cheeks, when she remembered his peremptory tone. It would be exciting to defy him and see if William de Lacey would receive her and if she could press him to give her an explanation of his conduct. She spurred her rather lazy palfrey to a gallop, and turned laughing as Oswin panted up behind. As the road entered into forest land, she noted the delicate tracery of the leaves above her. Coming sharply out of the sun, she was for a moment almost blinded and drew rein for a second to accustom her eyes to the different light. It was then that she saw the man leaning smiling against the bole of an oak tree. He did not move at their approach, and she gave a gasp of sudden surprise.

"Rolf—it is you."

"It is, lady."

"But I thought . . ." she broke off confused.

"You thought I was a prisoner," he finished smiling. "No, not for long. On the way back to Mountsorrel four of my men set upon my guards, and here I am free still but with a price on my head. Are you interested in acquiring it?"

She gave a laugh of pure goodwill. "You know I am not. Truly, Rolf, I am glad. I was disturbed for you."

"And I you, Lady Alys. Where are you riding with only one companion?" He came to her horse's head and lifted his hands to help her down.

"None of your business, Sir."

"It should be your husband's, lady. He is ill advised to let you ride near Mountsorrel, so poorly attended."

"Indeed it is to Mountsorrel that I ride."

His expression grew grave. "Lady, I do not counsel it. Please will you not dismount and be my guest for a short time."

She placed her head on one side and smiled crookedly. "The guest of an outlaw? The idea appeals to me. Help me down, Sir, please. Oh—you will find me stiff."

He lifted her in his strong arms, and she stumbled and almost fell, but he held her safe, while Oswin sprang down and led the two horses into the wood, after them.

"Careful, lady, the ground is rough and uneven, but my stronghold is not far." With a hand on her right arm he led her through the wood, pushing clear the low branches which impeded their way.

She gave a little cry of pleasure as they entered a small clearing. It was so well hidden, she would never have believed it so close to the road. Several men looked up at their approach. One was engaged in stirring a huge iron pot which had been suspended from two perpendicular poles over the fire. The other men appeared to be engaged in fashioning flights of goose quills for their arrows. Oswin gave them more than casual interest. The bow had been his joy, until forbidden to use it by Sir Geoffrey. The outlaws seemed a motley crew, roughly dressed, though clean enough at least outwardly, but they seemed to mean her no harm, and after acknowledging her presence with nods and grunts, continued about their business, several of them moving away, after staring curiously for one or two minutes. Rolf was obviously their leader. They treated him to an odd mixture of behaviour showing grudging respect and obedience. He led her to a felled log, and she sank down and spread her skirts womanlike, while he made a sign for the cook to bring her a cup of wine.

She accepted it, though looking at him with amusement. From whose cellar had it come or was it bought with money extracted from passers-by, by force? She could not tell. Oswin had wandered off to watch the fletchers at their task, and she put down the cup and questioned Rolf directly.

"So you think it unwise to visit Mountsorrel?"

"In your case I think it madness."

"You do not respect Sir William de Lacey?"

He was silent for a moment, turning away his head and she touched him lightly on the arm. "I am sorry if I hurt you."

His face was working when he turned back. "It is nothing, Lady Alys. It is over—my hurt, long ago."

"You knew him well?"

"Aye—I knew him well. I was his steward. When he called me a serf he lied. I am a free man and call no man master." He paused, then swallowed some ale from a pewter tankard. "Strange I should want you to know. You are practically a stranger, yet when he took me that day, I saw your eyes. You pitied me, you—the wife of a Baron."

"Is it so strange that I pitied one who was ill-treated? Norman or Saxon. It matters not."

"No it matters not, but it does to de Lacey. He has a strange sickness that man, ah well, tell you I must, for you must never go to him, or trust him unguarded. Swear to me."

"I will take your word."

"Well, as I said, I was steward of Mountsorrel for

FitzParnel. He was good to me in his way. My wife and I were happy there, and our little one grew strong and lovely. Then de Lacey came, and he saw my Joan. Very lovely she was, small and delicate, and he could not resist her."

"He took her?" the question was whispered. She knew well enough it was common practice on many a demesne, and Saxon serfs and men-at-arms accepted their lot with stolid patience.

"Aye he took her—not against her will. He did not need to do that. At first she tried to keep it from me but I knew. I accepted the situation," he shrugged lightly, "indeed there was naught else I could do. I saw clearly enough how he dealt with those who displeased him, and I had a little one to think of, my Blanchette. No, it was not that he cuckolded me. That I could have borne but from that first time, he began to kill her slowly."

"I don't understand."

His laugh was short, rather harsh. "No—you would not. He treated her well. I believe he gave her presents, though I saw none, but gradually, she began to realise that after the first time he had no further interest. He meant her no harm. He could not see that he had harmed her. She pined for him—then one day, she killed herself, opened a vein in her wrist. I was in time to hold her in my arms, and promise to care for Blanchette, though even then she appeared to have no interest in the child. I could tell her thoughts were only of him. It appears he had laughed at her when she told him she was to bear his child."

The story was so bald, told with a cold toneless quality, which made Alys shiver even in the warmth of the sun.

"I tried to kill him of course, I wounded him, then I fled with the child. I do not think he hates me. It is a game with him to pursue anything which hides or runs. With me it is a longing to see him finished because he dirties whatever he touches. This is why you must not see him again. I have taken an odd fancy to you. I would protect you from him, if I can."

She looked away from him across the clearing. "And your little girl?"

"My Blanchette is even more lovely than her mother. You would like to see her?"

"She is with you, here—in the woods?"

He nodded. "Aye. There was no help for it. She did live for a while with a friend, but she will soon be thirteen years old. I was worried about her. You will see why when you see her. Come." He reached down a hand to assist her to her feet and drew her towards a small lean-to hut, which the men had constructed of boughs covered with a rudely sewn together roof of deer-hide. He drew back a flap and motioned her to enter. She looked at him questioningly then stepped inside.

The light was dim in the rough shelter, but she could make out a bed of fern covered with cured skins. She drew closer and stared down at a slim girl, who was lying asleep. She had never seen such a beautiful child. She stirred faintly and half turned. The bone structure was finely drawn and delicate. A mass of tumbled fair hair covered the improvised pillow, but she was delicate. Alys could see that clearly, despite the dim light. Her hazel eyes took in at once the hectic flush which dyed the pale cheeks, and she bent down and placed her hand on the sweating brow. The girl opened her eyes, and stared up at her wonderingly.

"She has a high fever, Rolf."

"Aye—I know, she has never been strong. It is fine enough to keep her here with us now, but when winter comes, I shall worry. There is little shelter, and food is short."

"You must get an apothecary to make a cooling draught."

"Aye, one in Nottingham made some concoction for me. She seems better already. She knows me. I think she will recover, but she has been ill enough."

Alys smiled at the girl who gave a shy smile in answer. She was an exquisite little creature, but so fragile. Alys stepped out into the clearing and Rolf joined her, after speaking soothingly to his daughter.

"You thought she was too lovely to be within de Lacey's sight. Is that it?"

He nodded again. "Already he has noted her, though he doesn't realise who she is. I thought her best under my eye. Later I will try and make arrangements for her."

"Does she know—about her mother?"

"She knows and *his* part in it. I have kept nothing from her. Her beauty is childlike, but she is no fool, my Blanchette, she knows de Lacey for what he is."

Alys walked forward a little. "Rolf," she said at last, "you took a risk when you showed me your camp. Do you intend to set Oswin and myself free?"

"Of course."

"But why do you trust us?"

He smiled as she searched his lined face for her answer. "I am rarely wrong in my judgement of people. I did not think you a fool, Lady Alys . . . but . . ."

"You wondered why I ride to Mountsorrel without my husband's men-at-arms for escort?"

"I had not supposed from what I hear, that he would provide one, not for you to ride to Mountsorrel."

She smiled wryly. "I see you are kept well informed. Yes you are right, Rolf, it *was* a stupid idea. I cannot think why I should do it except that I . . . well, let that pass. I shall not ride any further. With your leave, I shall return to Birlstone. I would like to be home before sun-down."

"You should have plenty of time. If you wish I could send a man to guard you. You would not see him, but he would watch in case of need."

"No my friend. There is no need for one of your men to risk capture. Oswin and I will be safe enough on the main road."

"Yet *I* captured you."

"I allowed myself to be captured," then more seriously, "Rolf, if you need help for Blanchette, try to let me know. I will do what I can."

Again he looked at her searchingly then nodded. "So—thank you, My Lady. I shall not forget. Now you must go. I will call your attendant."

Oswin was staring down at a yew tree bow in his hand. One of the outlaws was laughing at him and holding out a small leather quiver of arrows.

"Take it, boy, you won it fairly."

"What is this?" Rolf questioned as he came up to the little knot of men. "Will, you rarely give away your property."

"The boy shot three arrows into the centre of the target. It was a wager. He is a promising archer."

Oswin turned and looked at her and Alys laughed. "Take it, Oswin, hide it somewhere close. He will never know of it from me, I promise."

The boy's face cleared and he ran to the horses, swinging the quiver over his left shoulder as he went.

Rolf lifted her into the saddle and led her by another path from the clearing. After a few yards, he stopped and pointed to the right. "This path joins another about a mile on. Turn to the right and it will bring you to the main road to Leicester. From there you can ride to Birlstone easily. It is a route to Mountsorrel, so watch your way."

"Thank you, Rolf, I will. Remember my words."

"Lady, I will. God keep you."

He lifted a hand in farewell as she urged her horse forward, Oswin following a few yards behind. Now that she had spoken with Rolf, she was all eagerness to return home. Her cheeks burned as she thought of her intended folly. If she were discreet, Sir Geoffrey would not know of the affair. She slackened speed a little and called back to Oswin to draw level. He complied at once, and she asked him what possibility there was of returning through the castle gate unrecognised.

"We must go separately, My Lady. I will take the horses in. I shall be scolded for being so long at the smithy, but they will merely think I was idling in the village. You must return as you left. The guard will have been changed by now. It will be getting dusk, he will notice nothing."

"Oswin, I will find a way to reward you."

"Lady, Hella lies in my hut, unlamed, apart from her sprain. But for you the foresters would have maimed her for ever. That is reward enough."

She smiled, "This lazy brute of mine has no speed, and I am anxious to reach that copse before dark."

"I will stay with you until you have changed, lady. I will not leave you alone."

Shr urged her ambling palfrey to greater speed, but met with little success, gratified to see at last the path of which Rolf had spoken, now ahead of her. Soon they would be out of the encircling trees and on the main road to Leicester. From there it was a safe enough ride to Birlstone, as the road was well frequented by travellers between the two towns. It was Oswin who called out the warning. She lifted her head to see a horseman coming close at a gallop. He was heading straight ahead for the Nottingham road and did not at first see them.

"Lady, turn back quickly into the trees. It is Sir Geoffrey."

Alys pulled on the rein sharply, and the grey whinnied in shrill protest. She could not be sure, but already the man had turned his horse. He had seen them, and immediately, turned down the side path to pursue. Alys was uncertain how to proceed. She could see now, it was indeed her husband, and alone. The dying sun glinted red on his short fair hair, he was not wearing mail, and had thrown back his short cloak of green wool for ease in riding. The sight of him was so unexpected, that she wavered. Of course later a reckoning would be demanded, but now, she only sought in a panic to avoid him, and turned back into the shelter of the trees. The grey had been frightened by the turn of events, and for once broke into a gallop. Oswin stayed behind her to guard her retreat. She had no idea of how she would escape. For the moment, she had only the instinct to ride away and keep riding. Behind her, she heard a peremptory shout of warning. Sir Geoffrey was now thoroughly roused, and his charger covered the ground, its hoofs thundering in a burst of speed. Oswin thought only of staying his furious master, and warding off any punishment he might bestow on his hapless wife. He reached for his only weapon. The grey goose flight sped through the air. Sir Geoffrey gave a gurgling cry and fell forward. The charger, feeling the slackening of control, shied nervously, and Sir Geoffrey fell with a crash, striking his head on a large boulder which bordered the pathway.

At his cry, Alys turned and pulled round her horse. She jumped from the saddle and ran to her husband's side. White and tense, Oswin sat still on his own mount, staring at his handiwork. The Baron lay so still, that a deadly cold hand touched Alys's heart. She lifted his head to her lap and strove to gauge the injury.

"Geoffrey—Geoffrey, oh God, what have I done?" Blood was welling over his mantle and she put her hand down to search for its source. Almost at once she was moved firmly aside and a pair of strong arms lifted the injured man to a sitting position.

"Oswin—go, do not stay. You can do nothing here. Go lad, I say, at once."

At Rolf's urgent call, Oswin stared briefly once at the little group then urged his mount forward in obedience to the older man.

"Quiet, lady do not be alarmed. It is a shoulder wound. He will soon regain consciousness. Lift his head onto your lap again. I will fetch water."

Alys placed a cold hand on her husband's brow, but his lashes did not flicker and she waited anxiously until Rolf returned with a rag soaked in water, and bathed the white face gently.

"So this is Sir Geoffrey de Courcelles in search of you?"

"I fear so. I did not expect him home until later in the week. Rolf, he will not die . . ."

"Nay, lady," the outlaw smiled grimly, "men do not

die of such wounds. The arrow has bitten deep into the flesh of the upper arm by the look of it." He probed gently, tearing away the velvet of the Baron's mantle to reveal the full extent of the injury. Alys turned away and shuddered as she saw the dark blood still ebbing from the wound made by the barbed arrow. "It will be better to summon a skilled surgeon from Leicester or Nottingham to remove the arrow head. He will make a cleaner job of it than I, though I have removed a few in my time. Ah, he is coming to."

Sir Geoffrey's lashes flickered open and for the space of one or two seconds, he stared blankly at the bearded face above him, then struggled in Alys's grasp to rise.

"Rest back a moment, Sir Geoffrey, you hit your head sharply, there is no great harm done."

Sir Geoffrey turned his head and Alys realised that he knew her at once, then he frowned slightly as though attempting to place the man's face in his memory.

"Who are you?" he said a trifle huskily.

"My name is of no significance. At the moment I act as a friend. Keep still and I will break off the shaft. A surgeon can deal with the rest."

Sir Geoffrey gritted his teeth as Rolf took the arrow firmly between brown fingers and snapped off the shaft, then padded the wound with the wet cloth. Alys knew with a sudden pang, that the action had given the Baron intense pain, for though he uttered no sound, his face had whitened and developed a pinched look round his nose and mouth. He attempted to raise himself and Rolf shook his head as she tried to prevent him.

"Your horse is standing by. He did not go far. I will secure him and help you into the saddle. You can ride?"

Sir Geoffrey nodded briefly, and she waited, supporting his weight against her shoulder, until Rolf returned. He said nothing, and she deemed it best to stay silent. He got to his feet as the outlaw leaned down a hand to assist him and swung himself clumsily into the saddle. Her own horse was cropping contentedly nearby, and she limped to her side and led her over to the two men. She was stiff from her cramped position on the ground and Rolf lifted her bodily into the saddle and gave her the reins.

"I will walk with you."

Alys thought Sir Geoffrey would protest, but he did not and she saw him sway momentarily in the saddle, and he seemed glad of the other man's assistance. If he were doubtful about his identity, he gave no sign. It seemed an age before they reached the main road and Alys watched anxiously as her husband rode slowly, but with dogged determination to keep going. When they reached the open road, he drew rein and leaned down to speak to his helper.

"Leave us now, friend. I shall do well enough."

Rolf smiled bleakly, "Truth to say, it were less dangerous for me, if I turned back now, but you are sure you can manage?"

"Quite sure. It is only an hour's ride to Birlstone. My own physician will attend me there. More of my men are combing the wood and roads nearby for Lady Alys. I shall be safe enough. They may possibly join us."

"Then God guard you both," Rolf stepped back and lifted his hand in farewell. The Baron leaned over and took her bridle rein as well as his own, and together they rode on to Birlstone.

✑ Chapter Seven

ALYS WATCHED anxiously as Ibrahim examined the wound and pursed his lips. Captain Roul had escorted Sir Geoffrey up the stairs of the keep and he was now looking pale but determined, leaning back against the pillows of their bed. Elfrida after one frightened glance had scuttled off for hot water and towels and Ibrahim ben Echtal had been summoned from his apartments, where he was busy concocting his herbal draughts. Sir Geoffrey looked up at Roul who stood awaiting orders."

"Find the boy, Oswin—and Roul, I want him alive."

"Yes, My Lord."

"Right, now leave me with Ibrahim."

The doctor turned to the chest behind him, where he had laid out his instruments. "I think it better, Lady Alys, if you went too. I will call you when I have finished. Sir Geoffrey is in no danger."

Alys's eyes flickered nervously to the knife which the Saracen was holding in the candle flame. "I would rather stay. Surely there is some way I can help."

"I think not. Please go."

Sir Geoffrey's voice was weak but testy, "Let her stay, Ibrahim. Do you think I shall make a fuss?"

"I did not think that for a moment," Alys said quietly.

Ibrahim shrugged philosophically. "As you wish. Could you support Sir Geoffrey by the shoulders?"

Alys sat on the upper end of the bed and drew her husband's shoulders against her breast. She bit her own lip as she saw the surgeon cut deep with his knife. Sir

71

Geoffrey's body went taut under her hands and she knew he was again gritting his teeth against the pain, then Ibrahim dropped the blood-soaked arrow head into a basin of water, and bathed the wound clean with a mixture of wine and water.

"He might have killed you had he wished. His aim was good, I think, merely to stop you in your tracks, not to end you."

"Perhaps he may live to regret that he did not," Sir Geoffrey said harshly, as Alys settled him back on the pillows, as Ibrahim completed his work of bandaging the wound. "Are you concerned about the boy's safety or mine?"

"A little bit of both, I think," Ibrahim said smiling. "Some wine, I think, Lady Alys, then I declare that our patient should do well enough."

"There is no danger, Ibrahim?" her question was urgent.

"Not in the slightest. The soreness will not improve his temper for the next few days, but he is quite safe."

"Thank you." She watched as he left the room, and then she turned unwillingly to meet her husband's sardonic gaze.

"I am truly sorry, Sir Geoffrey. I had no wish that you should be hurt as a result of my foolish escapade."

"That at least is an honest apology," he grunted sharply, as he eased himself on the pillows. "Don't be afraid. I did not for one minute think that you did, however it does not alter the situation in the slightest."

"No, I realise that. One thing only I will offer in our defence, we were returning home when you found us."

"I see, that was why the boy shot me."

She swallowed nervously, "I do not know why he did. He was afraid for me. He wished to give me time."

"And the outlaw—you know him?"

"I have met him before," she measured her words carefully in answer. "You will not hunt him down. He wishes us no harm, and has done me good service."

"That I can believe."

"You will not hang Oswin?"

"You heard my order. I want him alive."

"And then?"

"And then, I will consider." He smiled but a trifle frostily. "I think it would be wiser if you left me to rest for a while. I will send for you later. There is much to discuss—but not now."

She hesitated, but his eyes closed wearily and she knew there was no further point in remaining. She dropped a cool little curtsey and withdrew.

It was Elfrida who some hours later found her in her old private solar. It had seemed to be her only refuge from curious eyes in the whole of the castle.

"My Lady—it is Marian, Oswin's sister, she begs to see you."

Alys rose hastily from her chair. "Bring her in at once, Elfrida."

The girl's expression told her at once the news she dreaded to hear. She gathered the sobbing child close to her for a moment then drew her to a stool and gently forced her down onto it.

"So they have taken Oswin?"

Marian was too choked for a moment to answer, and she continued to sob in a dull hopeless fashion, from which there seemed no jot of relief. Elfrida shook her head over the girl's bowed shoulders. She forbore to comment on what she thought had been rashly dangerous behaviour, which had brought the boy to this. Alys waited silently until the storm was over the worst, and said quietly, "Does your mother know, Marian?"

"Yes, My Lady."

"Where is Oswin? Is he hurt?"

"They have taken him to the dungeons. I did not see him but Otho from the stables said there was blood on his garments and a bruise down one side of his face, but he was walking well enough when they brought him in. Oh, My Lady," the next words came in a stumbling rush, "you will plead with the Baron for him please . . ."

"Of course I will, Marian. Indeed I have already done so, but I will go and try again. I swear to you everything that can be done will be, if I have to go publicly on my knees and plead for him, I will not shirk it. Stay here with her, Elfrida. I will go down and see what I can discover."

"My Lady, you should not go down there," Elfrida said extremely shocked.

Alys did not answer. She made an imperative gesture for her nurse to stay where she was, then hurried from the room. The guard in the entrance room stared at her curiously as she brushed past him, but made no effort to detain her. She rarely now went below ground level, as her husband had made himself responsible for the castle stores, and so far the dungeons had remained uninhabited. Her soft shoes made little sound on the stone steps and her husband and Roul turned, surprised, as she rounded the last bend of the stairs and entered the large underground room, where her father had imprisoned refractory serfs to be charged with more serious offences in the manor court, and more frequently those who had displeased him personally in some minor infringement of rules. Baron Geoffrey's fair brows met in a frown of disapproval and he stepped forward to question her presence.

Alys momentarily ignored him. She stared beyond him to where Oswin was secured to the wall of one of the dungeon embrasures, his hands stretched cruelly wide and above his head, fastened by iron rings to two staples in the stone. He seemed calm enough. The bruise stood out clearly on his forehead and there were streaks of blood on his tunic. His eyes watched her warily, though he said nothing.

"What are you doing here, Madam?" the Baron's cold question cut across her thoughts. Already he appeared to have recovered from his weakness.

"I was seeking you, my lord. I had heard that the boy was taken and thought to find you here."

"I shall be returning to the Great Hall in a few moments. It would be more appropriate if you waited there."

"I was concerned about Oswin. Please, Sir Geoffrey, I beg of you. His fault was mine. Let the boy live."

"I had not thought to take his life."

His immediate reply came as a surprise and she turned open-mouthed to face him. He continued, "I had already come to the conclusion that the fault did not lie entirely with the boy. However Oswin knows full well the penalty he has incurred. I warned him not to take the bow into his hands again. He has defied me, and must lose his hands."

Alys gave a little cry of pity and moved towards the boy who had gone suddenly white and had closed his eyes, though he uttered no sound. Sir Geoffrey moved away from the dungeon and gestured his captain to leave them. Alys heard the man's heavy steps as he ascended the stair, and at her husband's curt command, went over to join him. She knew Oswin strained to hear what they said, but as her husband spoke to her in low tones, she kept her own answers as soft.

"You were riding to Mountsorrel." It was a baldly stated fact rather than a question.

"I intended to do so but . . ."

"The boy insists that you did not arrive there."

"No, that is true."

"You left the castle some time ago for a simple ride. Elfrida, when questioned, said you had gone some hours before I came to search for you."

"I . . . I was in the wood with the man Rolf. We were delayed."

"You ask me to believe that you accompanied an outlaw into the wood and stayed there an hour or more talking with him."

"I am telling the truth," she broke off embarrassed. "I know the tale sounds strange. I had met Rolf before when I—when we journeyed to Nottingham. He seemed kind. I trusted him. Indeed it was Rolf who counselled me not to ride on to Mountsorrel. Do you disbelieve me?"

He did not answer at once but stood searching her face intently. She had already found his habit of intense concentration on the features of his companions, unnerving and more so now, and found herself flushing guiltily under his scrutiny. Strangely, he did not answer her question, but followed with one of his own.

"Did you know that de Lacey asked for your hand in marriage on the death of your father?"

Her lips parted soundlessly. The question came as a complete shock. "No," she said, "I did not."

"He was a frequent visitor to Birlstone, an acknowledged suitor?"

She shook her head emphatically. "I had never set eyes on William de Lacey until I met him on my journey to Nottingham."

One fair brow arched in surprise and again she reddened, though he passed no comment. She could read his thoughts. On the death of her father she had become an heiress. Previously she had held no attraction for de Lacey with the possibility of her father remarrying and acquiring an heir. Her husband's cold contempt angered her. If the distasteful fact were true of de Lacey, it was no less so of his *own* decision to become her husband.

"If I were to die, de Lacey would find Birlstone an admirable possession. He holds Mountsorrel only in trust for FitzParnel."

"I am glad," she said icily, "that I appear to be of some value to both you gentlemen."

He ignored her cutting remark and looked full at her again, his blue eyes weighing her in the balance, and *she* was the first to draw aside her gaze.

"There is one way to make quite sure that de Lacey does not gain possession of Birlstone. If you were to give me an heir, should I die, the boy would be ward of the crown, and Birlstone would be his."

She drew back and dropped her eyes. She was near to tears but fought them back. "I know my duty, Sir Geoffrey," she said in a husky whisper, "my father impressed the sense of it well enough upon my mother. I will do what is required of me—when I can."

He came behind her and taking her shoulders in a firm clasp turned her towards the boy.

"Give me an heir within the year, and Oswin may keep his hands."

She struggled to turn but he held her steadily. Her lip trembled. "And if I fail?—it may not be possible."

"That would be unfortunate—for the boy." He turned her back to face him and lifted her chin with one hand. "If you manage to fulfil your part of the bargain by the second year, he may yet keep one hand. Need I go on?"

Tears were blinding her now, though she cried silently. She nodded her head.

"He will remain here until I decide otherwise."

"But he is chained like an animal."

"Exactly." He released her gently and she fell back a little once again, then recovered herself and went back to Oswin.

"My lady," he whispered, "you must not admit anything for my sake. You cannot save me."

"Do not fear, Oswin," she said quietly, "I *will* save you," then without once looking back, ran clumsily to the bottom of the stairs and away from both jailor *and* prisoner.

Dinner in the Great Hall was an ordeal to Alys, though Sir Geoffrey appeared his usual courteous self. He spent most of the meal discussing the merits of some new potion which Ibrahim had concocted and which he was determined to try on old Maude who lived at the mill. She was suffering badly with her chest after having a heavy cold, and her laboured breathing was affecting her heart. Alys only half listened to their talk. She was sorry for the old woman and would visit her, but her mind was abstracted. When she rose from the table, Sir Geoffrey politely excused her. As she had previously noted in the dungeons, he seemed almost to have completely recovered from the effects of his wound. She slipped away and gave herself to Elfrida's ministrations. Her nurse was inclined to scold, but one look at her former nursling's face, stilled her chattering tongue and she undressed her in silence, and let down the dark brown mass of hair, and relieved her over-wrought feelings by giving it a vigorous brushing. Wrapped in a furred bed-robe, another luxurious gift from her husband, Alys critically surveyed herself in the old iron mirror which had been her mother's. She looked pale but uninteresting. Her lips were trembling and there were dark shadows round her eyes.

It was thus Sir Geoffrey found her, and he signalled silently for Elfrida to leave them. Turning abruptly, Alys saw the arras drop into place behind the re-treating woman, and half rose. He took the mirror from her fingers and pushed her gently back onto her seat. His lips curved a little into an unaccustomed smile. She was so very determined to act the martyr and he was equally determined that this should not be. He tilted up her serious face, and kissed her tenderly. In all the months of marriage he had shown her no gesture of affection, other than the customary kiss of the marriage ceremony. She submitted, though her body grew icy cold and he saw alarm leap into her eyes. He said no word, but still smiling, gathered her into his arms and moved to the comfort of the bed, in which she had slept alone since their marriage night.

❧ Chapter Eight

ALYS AWOKE suddenly to find Elfrida bending over her, and bright sunshine flooding into the room from the unglazed window above her head. She stared a little vacantly at her nurse then turned to search for him. She was alone. Not even the mattress and pillows by her side gave evidence of his presence. He had stolen quietly away while she slept, and she saw by the position of the slanting sunbeams and the shadows, that it was late. She coloured and drew the covers around her more closely. Elfrida appeared not to notice her confusion. She seemed her old cheerful self.

"Good morning, Lady Alys. It is past ten. The Baron asked me to let you sleep, then bring some food up on a tray."

Alys turned her head and smiled faintly at the rich array; a tankard of brown ale, fine white bread, slices of cold beef. She realised that her hunger was sharp and nodded.

"Thank you, Elfrida. Leave the tray. I'll call you when I need you."

When the nurse had gone, she reached for a covering to drape her nakedness and stepped to the doorway. At the other end of the hall the scullions were setting up the trestle tables and singing a ballad as they worked. There was no sign of Geoffrey. She returned to her bed and climbing in, once more revelled in lazy freedom and reached out for the slices of bread and meat.

So he had gone and was already busy about the commonplace tasks of the day, but he had left her to dream and sent up food for her pleasure. She smiled again, a little secret smile, and bit deeply into the crusty slice. She *was* hungry, and simple food had never before tasted so good. Her smile faded a little as she recalled the delights of the past night, she who had dreaded so much becoming a woman and a wife. She had prepared herself for pain even brutality and fear, vague hints of her mother's unhappy experiences lurking in her remembrances, but it had not been like that. He had laughed at her determination to suffer and endure. Geoffrey de Courcelles was a skilled and experienced lover, and he did not lack patience. Quietly and slowly, he had waited until she was ready to respond to his ardour, and he had been amazed himself, at her answering passion. At first frigid and tense, she had relaxed under his gentleness, and learned to give the whole of herself without restraint. Alys had waited long for someone to break down the dam of reserve she had built around her heart, and once breached, it was swept away on the tide of her happiness. He loved her—the plain brown girl of Birlstone. It was incredible but true. He was hers, and he could give her ecstacy she had not known existed. Now he had thought of nothing but her comfort.

Alys did not hurry over the meal. She allowed herself to remain in the warm tender delight of her new found love. She was unwilling to break the moment, fearful that its splendour would pale or fade in the cold light of day. When it was time to dress, she did not send for Elfrida, preferring to deal herself with the refractory hooks and troublesome fastenings. No one must intrude on her tiny heaven of privacy, not just yet. She chose her finest gown of green, the colour he had chosen for her, though it was still morning and an unusual choice. She lifted her old scratched mirror and wondered guiltily if her confessor would note the changes in her appearance, the warm curve of her lips, the brightness of her hazel eyes. Would he know that she was a woman suddenly, completely in love? She had heard him many times talk with sternness of carnal desires, but she was a wife, it could be no sin to love her husband with all of her heart. She checked for a moment as her thoughts sped to Oswin, chained to the stone of the dungeons below her. She must spare time to go to him and assure herself that he had been fed and given water, for he could no longer acquire these necessities for himself. That could come later, but first she must find Geoffrey.

She found him in the bailey discussing some point of defence with his two captains. He looked up at her approach and gravely waited for her to come close. She had always found herself somewhat tongue-tied in his presence, he always had the effect of making her feel clumsy and awkward, even a little foolish, but today she found herself quivering with an emotion she could not comprehend. She had always before been able to find words to answer his courteous treatment of her, but now she experienced a shyness too intense to express her thoughts aloud. He greeted her coolly and politely, as he always had done, enquired if Elfrida had obeyed his instructions and brought food to their apartment. He expressed gratification that she had slept well and his blue eyes dwelt appreciatively on her slim figure in the green kirtle but she experienced a cold douche of shock. He appeared completely unchanged. There was no warmth in his eyes, in the tone of his voice consideration and concern for her welfare, but no depth of affection betrayed itself. She was stung to search his countenance in vain for evidence of his answering delight in her surrender. He gave no sign. Already she felt his mind had passed on to other matters, though he continued to give her his attention while she remained. He made no effort to dismiss his officers, but appeared to be waiting quietly to resume his business. She did not understand. A cold little shiver of fear passed through her body. Had she been mistaken? Had he no real love for her, and had his tenderness of the night been merely consideration for her inexperience? She told herself that it was merely the presence of others. When they were alone, he would show his true affection for her, but again she peered at him, bewildered, hurt. He answered her scrutiny with an air of courteous puzzlement, and she excused herself, smiled at the captains and withdrew from them. When she turned at the castle entrance to look back at them, he appeared to have forgotten her and was once more engrossed in his plans for the strengthening of the fortifications.

She entered the entrance room of the keep, hesitated for a moment and then descended the steps to the dungeons. A man-at-arms was watching at the entrance, but he made no move to halt her, and she went to Oswin, whose eyes brightened at the sight of her. In the dim light, she thought he looked wearied and strained. He eased himself in the shackles, but his anxiety was all for her.

"Lady Alys, he did not hurt you?" the question was urgent.

She paused in the act of filling a panikin with water.

"No—Oswin, do not disturb yourself, he has not hurt me in the slightest."

He swallowed thirstily, and her heart was touched with pity at his inability to help himself. If she were not able to keep her part of the bargain, he might never again be able to eat like a human being, but permanently incapacitated, he would be forced to live on what others chose to throw him in pity. Serf or no, she knew that Oswin's was a proud spirit, and once again she determined to do all in her power to aid him. She questioned him about the guard's treatment.

"They have fed me, lady. Do not worry. It is just that sometimes," he paused and coloured, "I thirst and I cannot . . ."

"I will see that you are not neglected," she cut him short, "I will visit you whenever I can and I will convey news of you to your family. Marian came to see me. She was worried but I will visit your mother and see that she does not starve. Do not fret."

As she moved to go, he called after her, one despairing cry, "My Lady—my hands—when will they . . ."

She returned, but did not meet his eyes as she said hurriedly, "The Baron has not yet decided. I know it is hard to live in fear, but keep up your spirits. I am trying all I can to save you from *that* fate. Now I must leave you."

He nodded and rested back against the wall. Satisfied that Sir Geoffrey had not wreaked his anger on his beloved mistress, he was prepared now to await stoically, what fate had in store for him.

Alys could never have said afterwards how she lived through the remainder of the day. She saw little of Geoffrey, who seemed obsessed with a determination to make Birlstone impregnable. At dinner she ate little, though he engaged her in pleasant conversation, but she looked for one glance of true affection, one sign that she had not judged his ardour of the previous night incorrectly.

As the days passed, the hurt diminished, but did not disappear. She knew now that she was incapable of inspiring him to return her love. He was polite, considerate—the perfect lover, or so he seemed, gentle and kindly, but unmoved. He did not appear to be aware of her silent cries for understanding. Perhaps he did not know the lonely hours she spent weeping in her apartment, or the soft appeals she made at her prie-dieu, for the Virgin to grant her his love, if only in part, or failing that, the solace of a child to comfort her loneliness.

Perhaps the Virgin was not deaf to the cry from the heart of the unhappy girl. To Alys's delight she gradually became aware that at least one of her prayers had been answered. She could not be sure, and until she was, she must speak no word. It would be disastrous if his hopes were raised in vain, and though she refused to admit her motive, even to herself, she knew that if he became aware of her condition, he might withdraw his attention completely. The thought of this, she could not bear. She loved him completely and without conditions. The time he spent with her, she locked in her heart to remember, and though she spoke nothing to him of her secret longings, she was content, while he was at Birlstone, to have him within her sight. If he knew, he might leave her. The castle was now well defended. There was nothing to hold him here, only the desire to creat an heir.

It was one day about a month later, that she returned to the castle from a visit to the manor farm. Even in this early stage, she had refrained from riding, but it was not far and she would have found the exercise pleasant, had it not been for the complaints of Elfrida who hated walking. Alys's new found pleasure in it, had not met with her approval, and Alys had not yet even divulged to her, the reason for her determination not to ride. It was a true Autumn day, the sun's faint warmth lighting up the trees of the forest to a fire of beauty, the leaves crisp and snapping under their feet. The nights would soon draw in very early and Sir Geoffrey would be forced to spend more time within the castle walls. She hugged the thought to her, as she entered the main gate. The ostlers were leading two strange horses to the stables. She cast them only a casual glance, though they appeared to have been ridden hard, for the grooms led them gently and she noted the lathering of sweat on their heaving flanks. They had visitors then but it could be no one of importance to ride with no escort, and neither horse was richly caparisoned. As she entered the keep, she met Alain Guilbert, Sir Geoffrey's squire. The young man apologised as he almost knocked into her in his haste.

"Your pardon, lady. I was about to go to the stables to attend to the care of the messengers' horses. I did not notice you. My thoughts were elsewhere."

"The horses were being correctly handled, Alain. You seem concerned, who is our visitor?"

"Two messengers from the Welsh Marches. Sir Geoffrey is receiving them now. It seems there is trouble."

A cold finger touched Alys's heart. Already she guessed at the worst. When he summoned her, the two men had been taken off half dead to the kitchens where they could be fed, and allowed to drowse in the warmth. His tone was brisk.

"There is trouble in Gwyndd. I must leave early in the morning. If I set off at once, I should possibly be able to return before the worst weather sets in, though snow in the West falls earlier than here. I shall take Roul. He is the most experienced of my captains, and I need him. Walter can be trusted to serve me well here. Your defences are in order and supplies should last through to the Spring. Since you are recovered of your hip disability, I will take leave to relieve you of Ibrahim's care. You are all well enough?"

It was a statement rather than a question. For one moment she hesitated, then memories of her own mother's repeated miscarriages kept her from telling him of her condition. He would be back soon enough, then she would be sure, and it would be time to tell him. She nodded quietly.

He continued, "Good, I leave you in Elfrida's care. She loves you well, as do all the servants. Gilbert knows my wishes and will obey, I think."

"There is danger for you?" her voice was low, but she strove to sound calm.

He checked suddenly and turned his candid blue eyes on her face. "I think not. My castle at Gwyndd is remote and sometimes attacked by small bands of the Welsh. They have been troublesome of late, my castellan informs me. It is time I taught them a lesson. I shall take a company of picked men. The matter will soon be settled. As soon as that is done, I shall return. This year I wish to spend Christmas at Birlstone."

She flushed slightly at his implied reason, then turned from him, as he appeared to have completed his instructions.

She slept little that night, lying by his side content to have him so close. He was not wakeful, but slept peacefully enough, but he woke early and called for Alain to arm him, after eating a hasty meal. She dressed hurriedly herself, determined to see him ride off and herself offer him the stirrup cup, as she had so many times done for her father.

He turned unexpectedly as she entered the hall. "One last instruction." He slapped down on the oaken table a small key. "This is to Oswin's fetters. You may release him from the dungeon, but he is not to leave the castle. Find him employment in the stables or the kitchens." She picked up the key wonderingly. Weeks ago, Oswin had been released from his cramped position and was now fettered by one ankle only to a ring in the wall. Now she was to free him completely.

"If he should escape?" she asked quietly, "I have few men to pursue him."

"He will not do so." His answer was confident, "Not while you stay at Birlstone. The boy's concern is for you. That is well, provided he leads you into no danger. No, the boy will be here when I return. I trust you see that he is so, remembering well our bargain."

"I will do so."

"Good." He bent his head and kissed her full on the lips. She longed to fling her arms around him and beg him to stay, or plead to accompany him, but she held back and forced a tight smile.

"Fare you well, Sir Geoffrey. I will do your bidding at Birlstone until you return." She knew any pleading she made would be in vain, and the one lever she had to compel his attention, she would not use. She accompanied him to the bailey and watched while the company of men rode from her across the drawbridge, then she strained her eyes until she could no longer see the bannerets at the top of the lances nor the swirl of dust rise into the air behind the last horseman. She gave a little sigh and turned back into the keep but was arrested by the soft patter of Father Anselm's sandals as he came towards her from the gate.

"I am too late then," he panted as she smilingly greeted him, "I hoped to bid Sir Geoffrey 'God speed'. I heard in the village he intended to leave today, but did not think it would be so early."

"When my husband determines on a course of action, he wastes no time," she said a little bitterly, "but you are welcome, Father. Come in and eat with us."

She must have betrayed her feelings somewhat, for he looked at her sharply and she turned her face away and led him up to the solar. Elfrida brought ale, for he disliked wine, and he leaned back and enjoyed it. It had been a hectic walk and he was running to fat. His breath was becoming short. He must look to his habits. It would never do to become too lazy to work well. The little priest was a conscientious shepherd of his flock, and he had sincere affection for Lady Alys. His round eyes looked down inquisitively at the key held tightly in her hand.

"I am to release Oswin," she said, her eyes following his, and the priest's face brightened.

"Then Sir Geoffrey has forgiven him?"

"Not exactly," she hesitated and sought to avoid the priest's eyes, then knowing him to be her friend, and confessor she quietly told him of her pact with the Baron. He was very gentle and showed his concern.

"You must not blame yourself nor charge Sir Geoffrey with unnecessary cruelty. He does less than many men in his position would have done."

"I know it."

"There is plenty of time. You are young and strong. I will pray that you might conceive soon."

She smiled faintly and touched his calloused hands. "I think you need not concern yourself over Oswin's fate, Father Anselm."

"Then you are with child?"

"Yes, but it is early days yet, and I have kept it to myself. When he returns, it will be soon enough to raise his hopes."

"Then why do I find you so unhappy? He is cruel to you?"

"No, Father."

"You love him?"

"Yes, Father, with all my heart."

"Then why so cold?"

"He goes from me."

"And will return soon enough."

"Aye," she sighed and rose, "he will come back. He treats me well but I want more than that." Her words came with a sudden rush. "I am an ungrateful child of Mother Church, Father. I have been granted so much more than I dared to hope for. A husband considerate of my welfare, relief for my crippled hip, and now— my child, is it so much that I ask that my husband should love me? My mother did not ask such a boon, indeed I do not think she wanted it, but I love him so, and he is kind. Do not misunderstand—he does not neglect me," she hid her face to hide the heightened colour in her cheeks, "indeed he gives me much pleasure, more than perhaps is good for me to delight in, for I have often listened to your counsel as my confessor."

"My child," his voice was very gentle, "you should know well that there is nought sinful in a wife's submission to her husband, nor in her happiness in the performing of her wifely duty. As to your husband's apparent lack of affection, men are ever thus. Passion they expend in other directions. If he is kind to you, you must find your fulfilment in that alone. Be patient, child. When you give him a son, he will have cause to bless you."

"It is as you say, Father. My mother, I know, had more blows than kind words from my father. I have no right to ask more than I am granted. You will not speak of my feelings—not to him."

"Of course not. It was as if the seal of the confessional were on your words. Come, child, delight your eyes in Oswin's pleasure at his freedom. That at least, you can do."

⇒ Chapter Nine

"My lady, are you alone? I wish to speak with you urgently." Alys was relieved to hear Oswin's voice and she bade him enter. He had been gone some time to see his mother in the village, and she was anxious about him. In spite of Sir Geoffrey's strictures on his leaving the castle, Alys had allowed him one or two illicit visits to his mother, on his assurance, that he would return quickly. She did not know how he left the castle without being challenged by the guard and she did not enquire. She felt for the lonely woman in the manor cottage and she trusted Oswin to obey her, but this morning he had been some hours away and she frowned a little as he entered.

"You have been too long, Oswin. You must not be missed. Sir Geoffrey would punish you and be displeased with me if he learns that his instructions have been ignored."

"Lady, I was delayed. You are sure you are alone?" His tone was eager, and she looked up at him surprised.

"Quite alone. Elfrida is in the kitchen. What is it?"

"There is one who would speak with you privately."

"I do not understand. No one in the castle is barred from seeking me out."

"I did not say one from the castle, lady." His answer was again cautious.

She started as she caught his meaning, her eyes widening. "Rolf . . ."

"Hush, lady," he nodded smiling. "I could take you to him. I have smuggled him into the bailey. Will you speak with him?"

She rose at once and prepared to follow him, but first she donned a thick cloak, for already the first snows of January had fallen and it was bitterly cold. Already her pregnancy had betrayed itself, and the manor rejoiced with her at the promise of her first child in the Spring. Only Geoffrey did not join them. She had had one letter from him three months ago, saying that he would be longer than he hoped, but still with her before the Winter, but since then, there had been no word from him. Obviously bad weather in Wales had prevented his return, and she must wait awhile before telling her news. Elfrida had fussed and clucked over her once the secret was out, anxious to ensure that during the critical early months she would be careful, but despite minor discomforts, her pregnancy had followed a normal course, and Alys felt as well as ever she had been. She left her apartment with Oswin and followed him to the stables. She was puzzled as to what reason Rolf might have to risk capture by visiting Birlstone. His need was urgent, that was very plain.

It was dark in the stables but chilly after the warmth of her apartment. Gradually she grew used to the gloom, and saw the outlaw's sturdy form against one of the mangers. He came forward at once to take her out-stretched hands.

"You are welcome, Rolf. How can I help you?"

Even in the dimness she glimpsed his answering smile. "Lady Alys, I knew you would listen to me and I had no one else to turn to."

"What is it—Blanchette?"

"You have guessed it. The child will be ill if she remains in the forest with us. Her cough is worsening, and she grows frailer each day. I dare not leave her in sight of de Lacey. Would you take her for a while into your service? Here at Birlstone, she could be safe. Oswin tells me Sir Geoffrey is away."

She nodded. "Three months gone, into Wales. I doubt now if he can be back before the Spring, but do not be afraid to leave her with me. He will understand."

"You are sure?"

"Of course," laughter was audible in her voice, "soon Elfrida will need extra help. I am to have a child."

He grasped her hand and squeezed it in his happiness. "I am glad for you. You keep well?"

"Well enough, Rolf, but I shall be pleased to greet my husband's return."

"He knows?"

"Not yet. Pray God I give him an heir for Birlstone. Now, what is best to be done? Do you know Oswin's cottage?"

"Aye. I have waited days for him to visit his mother. I had heard he was free." He smiled grimly. "Your serfs gossip freely in the ale houses and we outlaws know well what happens at the manor. I trusted only Oswin with my message, but I had not known he was forbidden to leave the castle precincts."

"Then take Blanchette there. Marian, Oswin's sister,

can bring her to the castle as a new seamstress. If she cannot sew, she can learn."

"Blanchette is a good needlewoman, well taught by her aunt."

"That is well. I have many gowns which need altering. Trust her to me, Rolf. Do not fear."

"De Lacey does not visit here?"

"He does not. As you know my husband has no love for him."

"Then I bless your name, lady, for coming to my assistance. Without your aid, she cannot survive the rigours of the Winter."

"Send her to me and keep yourself close. In the Spring I will send word when you can see her again. Now go with Oswin, before one of the grooms returns, and tattles of your presence."

He stooped and kissed the tips of her fingers, then he was gone. She stood for a moment until it was clear to follow, then returned to her apartment.

Alys was once more alarmed at the frailness of Rolf's daughter when Marian brought her to the castle. Her delicate beauty had blossomed since the Spring, and Elfrida muttered low in her throat at sight of her. True it was, she was a sight to turn the head of any man, but for all her fragility, Alys was to learn that the girl had wisdom above her years. She leaned against the doorpost coughing harshly, dark rose colour flooding her cheeks with the exertion. The journey from the village and the ascent of the steep stairs of the keep was for the time, too much for her, and she was unable to speak. Alys's heart was touched with pity for her thinness. The bones seemed like those of a bird. When at last she controlled the paroxysm, she came forward to her benefactress.

"My father has told me of your kindness, lady. It is to be hoped that I may prove to be of assistance," the voice was surprisingly low and mature, a faint trace of huskiness heightening its charm.

"You are welcome, Blanchette. Take off your cloak and come to the fire."

"My father tells me you need a seamstress. I think you will find me truly skilful."

"Later will be time to find you work. Rest, you are tired."

"It is the cough. It has worsened with the falling of the leaves. It is over now. My father frets more than he need, but he was anxious I should not remain in the open."

"I think it most unwise. It is only sensible you should come to us." Little more was said and Blanchette settled into the life of the castle with no more ado. Despite Elfrida's forebodings, she was a willing and reliable worker. Day after day her low contralto voice, so much in contrast to her fair delicacy, could be heard singing as she went about her tasks with a will. Her skill with the needle had not been exaggerated and not only was she able to alter Alys's gowns, but to fashion new ones which carried a boldness of cut and design which delighted both mistress and nurse. During the afternoons when Elfrida loved to doze, the two younger women would sit by the fire in the solar, over their needlework, and it was then, to the younger girl, that Alys could confide her fears and longings.

"I have long learned to take people as they are," Blanchette said gravely. "During my time in the forest, I had little to do but mark the motives and actions of men. My father's life depends on his judgement of those who cross his path. Some are to be trusted, others will betray without a twinge of conscience, but it is their frustrations which I was able to observe clearly. Some missed their homes and families, and would risk death for a sight of them, others were frankly glad to shed their responsibilities. All of them needed women—even my father. I soon realised their physical need was not to be confused with love."

"That I *too* have learned," Alys said bitterly.

"You may be wrong. Some men show affection more clearly than others. Did your father love your mother truly?"

"No—he made her life a misery, and rejoiced in his freedom when she died."

"My father loved my mother, but could not show her fully—so she turned to another."

"De Lacey."

"He is a strange man. I have watched him many times when I lived with my aunt. He *can* show his love easily and with charm. Few women can resist him. It is not his fault he tires of them so quickly."

"But you blame him for your mother's death."

"No." Blanchette's tone was decided. "Her tragedy was completely her own. She loved him and could not live without him. I blame no one for that."

Alys was embarrassed to ask her a question but Blanchette was quick to sense her curiosity. "You think I too was charmed by him, that it is my father only, who wishes to keep me clear of him. Is that what you are thinking?"

"I . . . I was not sure . . ."

"No, Lady Alys. I do not wish to belong to de Lacey—or to any man."

"But what will you do? There will be a day when your father can no longer protect you."

The blue eyes turned away and Blanchette was silent for a while. "I do not know what I shall do. I had thought to become a bride of Christ but I . . . I do not know."

"Your father does not wish it?"

"It is not that. Of course he would rather I remain in the world and perhaps find a husband and have children, but he would not forbid it. No—it is not for that reason that I hesitate. I cannot explain easily. Lady Alys, do not be angry with me when I say that I know men look at me with desire. It has always been so. I do not wish to enter the cloister to run from my fear of men though I know it here, that I do not wish to become a wife and I fear to become a mother." She touched her heart and then broke off her serious tone with a low laugh. "You will think me vain and stupid, lady."

"I do not think so at all." Alys rose. She had detected a note of panic in the other's voice she had never known before. The lovely eyes carried a haze of violet, but were vacant, as though she looked into the future and feared what she saw, then she bent to her task once more and Alys sought out some embroidery thread for her advice.

No news came from Sir Geoffrey and Alys set herself each day to see his instructions were obeyed to the letter. Gilbert no longer seemed resentful in his tone. He was anxious to receive her praise and courted it. She smiled thinly as she realised how different it was to be married to a strange and powerful Baron. The steward was determined she would find no fault with his duties, on his master's return. She resolutely told herself that the rosy flush in Blanchette's cheeks was due to improvement in her condition and not to the harsh dry cough which still persisted in spite of Elfrida's well tried remedies. Alys wished that Ibrahim were here that she might seek his advice, for though Blanchette never complained, it was obvious that the slightest exertion fatigued her beyond the normal for a girl of her age. Alys herself had felt so much better since Ibrahim's care of her that even the increasing heaviness of her advancing pregnancy caused only a slight return of her awkwardness of gait, and left her only momentarily exhausted after climbing the stairs. She was delighted to find herself now undisturbed by bouts of dizziness and nausea her mother had endured. She obeyed Elfrida's strictures to the letter, for the child was important to her happiness. Its safety must be guarded at all costs, and she forced herself to rest when commanded and resisted the temptation to ride in the cold, sharp air of the mornings. In her quiet happiness, she was all unprepared when the blow fell.

Walter one day came himself to the solar, his face grave. "My lady, I came myself to seek you out without concerning another in our decision. Sir William de Lacey has sent a messenger ahead with a polite request that you admit him with a small retinue. He wishes to see you."

Alys had dismissed Elfrida at his request and regarded him now with troubled eyes. "I do not know what is best, Walter. Sir Geoffrey is no friend of de Lacey. I fear he would not approve of him entering Birlstone."

Walter's answer was blunt. "My Lady, I do not advise a blunt refusal. De Lacey has a good force, and your own lord is not here to defend you."

"You think there is danger?"

The captain shrugged, "There is no need to anger him. The messenger tells me he is attended only by six men. There can be no harm in receiving him courteously."

"Very well, Walter, there is to be no word spoken about the presence of the seamstress Blanchette here in the castle. Make this plain. Am I understood?"

"Yes, lady. I will see to it."

"Then go. Admit Sir William and convey him to the Great Hall. I will prepare myself."

When he had gone, she frowned slightly. She had no wish to see de Lacey. What could she say to the man? Her own foolishness in ever having been charmed by him irritated her. His insolence in seeking her out when her husband was not present, angered her, but she judged it wiser to be ruled by Walter. She would receive him coldly but politely. Surely Sir Geoffrey could not then censure her for such a course of action. She sought out Blanchette and Elfrida, changed her attire and repaired to the hall to await her visitor, having bidden Blanchette keep herself hidden.

He was as handsome as ever, his fur lined riding cloak thrust back to reveal a surcoat of scarlet velvet, the wide sleeves themselves lined with the fur of his cloak. There was no trace of embarrassment on meeting her for the first time since his cruel action in publicly wearing her favour at the tournament, rather his handsome face wore only an expression of grave concern for her welfare.

"I am grateful that you agreed to see me, Lady Alys. I feared that you might wish to remain in seclusion at such a time. However your decision gives me added pleasure, that you should count me as your friend." His lips brushed the tips of her fingers and she stiffened slightly, as his grey eyes raked over her figure as he stood up to face her. Colour flooded her face at her condition.

"You are welcome to Birlstone, Sir William. Will you come to the fire. You must be frozen after the ride. Perhaps I may offer you wine. I hope it will be to your taste."

She seated herself in a carved chair to the right of the fireplace and waved him to a seat opposite. A servant offered him wine which he accepted, his eyes still taking in her appearance. Pregnancy had not affected her features, though there was maturity now in the steadiness of her gaze and in the full curve of her lips. He sought for traces of strain but found none.

"You must call on me at all times in your need, Lady Alys," he said at last, his tone warm with sympathy, "I have ridden from Nottingham and came at once to offer my condolences."

Her hand was arrested in the action of offering her goblet to the servant. She stared at him blankly.

"I do not understand you, Sir. You were kind to come, but I am at a loss to know your reason."

His eyes caught hers and were held. His eyebrows swept up in interrogation, then he looked away. "My Lady, I regret . . . I had no idea you were unaware . . . Forgive me, I should not have come."

One hand gripped tightly the arm of her chair. "You bring ill tidings, Sir William. I have had no word. Please I beg you—do not keep me in suspense now."

"Lady Alys, can it be that you have not heard of the Prince's defeat on the Welsh border? Your husband fought bravely, so I heard, but alas, the English force have been thrown back from the Marches."

"I have had no word from my husband. If you have news please tell me."

He stood up and paced from her the length of the hall, then turned suddenly, flinging back his cloak with an unconscious grace of movement, which had been long practised in earlier years.

"I see you have promise of an heir."

"Sir William—do not spare me. My husband is injured is that it?—Dead?" the last word was but a whisper but she leaned forward in her chair, her eyes appealing, and her voice carried across the space between them.

"Aye, lady—or so I heard."

She placed one hand on her heart and wondered dully why it did not cease to beat. Rather it seemed to beat with increased vigour. The knuckles of the other hand whitened, as it grasped the chair. She spoke no word, and he did not seek to break the silence. She had withdrawn into herself, the suddenness of the pain for a while numbing her consciousness.

"I will call your woman and withdraw," he said at last. "Forgive me, lady, that mine were the lips that gave you such pain. I had no conception that you were unprepared. My information was gathered from the Prince's court at Nottingham. Naturally I deemed you had been informed by a messenger from your husband's castle at Gwyndd."

"Tell me all you know please," each word was forced but steady, "please sit down and tell me."

"The Welsh Prince Llewellyn attacked the garrison at Ruabon. Baron Geoffrey de Courcelles led a sortie to relieve the castle. He was wounded and did not return to Gwyndd. The Prince later had word he had died of his wounds. The Welsh Prince offered his sympathy at our loss and expressed his admiration for your husband's chivalry. He declared that it would have been a privilege to have held such a man prisoner. I am deeply sorry."

"Thank you."

There seemed little to say. He waited for his dismissal, a faint frown creasing his brow. He had not deemed her so loyal. The marriage had been one of convenience, arranged so he thought against her will. Doubtless she was feeling the shock of widowhood and felt insecure. She was with child too—he had not known of that. It was an added complication. The blow once over, she would mend her life and take a new husband.

She rose suddenly and came towards him. "Do not blame yourself, Sir William, that you were the one to tell me. I shall ever be grateful for your sympathy. Some delay has obviously overcome my messenger. Doubtless Alain de Guilbert will send more definite tidings soon. Now, if you will excuse me."

"I understand. You will remember—that I am your friend if you need me."

"I will remember your words, Sir William, but I am well attended here and I am sure the Prince will arrange for my affairs and send word of his wishes."

He bowed and prepared to take his leave. "One query before I go, Lady Alys. I have sought news of an escaped serf. You may be able to help me."

"Indeed, Sir?"

"You will remember when we met, I was able to relieve you of the presence of a thieving rogue."

"I recall the incident. I thought you had him under lock and key or had hanged him out of hand."

Sir William's tone was silky, "Unfortunately, he slipped through my hands again, through the criminal negligence of my guards."

"I am sorry," she smiled a little bitterly, "but you can hardly imagine that the man might have sought refuge at Birlstone."

"Not the man, My Lady—he had a daughter."

"I see." She volunteered no interest but he continued. "She is a very lovely creature, by name Blanchette. You will understand, since she is mine, I have a wish to have her returned to Mountsorrel."

"That is understandable."

"You have had no strangers in the village, to your knowledge?"

"None I have heard of."

"Should you hear of the girl's whereabouts you will send me word?"

"Sir William, under the circumstances, I am not likely to concern myself with the fate of a village girl. I am sure your men are more capable of such work than I." Her words cut like a lash and reminded him of the continued discourtesy of his intrusion into her sorrow. He recalled his good manners and again bowed low. Assuring her once more of his sympathy and desire to be of service, he took his leave of her.

Dry-eyed, she called as many of the retainers and servants as she could gather together immediately, into the Great Hall, and told them briefly the news she had heard.

"We must assume for the moment at least, that the news is true, but I ask you to continue with your individual tasks as your Lord would have wished. You may go."

It was then and then only that she took herself to the chapel and slipped to her knees before the altar. Even then she was not granted the relief of tears. Over and over she repeated the prayers for the dead, mechanically without thought, without hope, and it was there that Blanchette found her, and dropping to her knees at her side, placed a comforting arm across the bowed shoulders. No words were said and they remained together in silence.

"I cannot go on without him," Alys said at last in a cold brittle little voice. "God cannot ask it of me. Until he came, my life was barren, now all that was given, has gone. Even though he did not grant me his heart, I had hoped that when I placed a son in his arms, he would turn to me. Now there is nothing to hope for—nothing."

"Lady Alys, how can you say that? Do you not bear his child—an heir or heiress to Birlstone? Can you say there is naught to hope for?"

Alys turned blankly to stare at her, as though at first she did not comprehend, then she fell forward into the other girl's arms and sobbed as if her heart would break. Half crouching, Blanchette held her to her own heart and waited until the spasm was over then she spoke briskly.

"Lady Alys, you must be strong. There will be many who will seek to rule here at Birlstone. Within days they will come seeking you as a bride and with you, the lands which are yours—yours to see that your child inherits. You must choose wisely and resist any effort at coercion to force you into an unsuitable match, even from court circles."

Alys nodded slowly and deliberately and turned just once, back towards the altar. She moved her lips in a silent vow. She would protect Geoffrey's child with all the strength and power within her. Blanchette was right, danger to the child's interests would now lie ahead, and it was for her to use a woman's cunning to see that she was not enmeshed in a web of self seeking intrigue. She rose to her feet and smiled at Blanchette.

"Do not fear, my friend. I am myself again. I know what you say is true. My child is all that matters. For him," she smiled faintly, "or her, I will fight to the end to ensure his well-being. Now let us go about our work. The men must see that I am able to control them, or they will become slack about their duties again."

Chapter Ten

ALYS'S FOREBODINGS were not at once to come to pass. Almost at once she expected to receive a command from the Prince to hand over the control of the castle to some baron he favoured. She was surprised to receive a visit from the Regent himself three days later. Again, she marvelled at his courteous treatment of her.

"Lady Alys," he said gravely, "it distresses me that so soon I must offer you my sympathy. As you know, I have had only partial news from the Marches, but it seems true enough that Sir Geoffrey was slain. His little troop was cut off in one of the passes and until I receive an official report from his squire or one in authority, I can tell you little more than you appear to know already." He was seated in the carved chair in the hall, one booted leg thrust out towards the blaze in the hearth. He had declined to take refreshment and declared his intention of continuing his journey to London, almost immediately.

"I am honoured and grateful that you should come, Sire," Alys said quietly, "I am distressed that I had no word of your visit and was ill prepared to receive you."

"My dear, I merely came to assure you of my support."

She waited in an agony for him to declare his policy, but he continued to repeat polite and kindly expressions of his regret for her loss, and at last took his leave. Before mounting, he bent low to her ear and said quietly:

"If you need assistance, send at once to me. Do not wait or fear that I shall do aught but in your best interests and those of your child. I held Geoffrey in high regard, indeed he was one of a very small company I deemed my trusted friends. Please remember." She looked up into the handsome Plantagenet face and gave a small answering smile.

"Sire, I will remember. Bless you for your comfort. God speed you on your way."

As he rode forth, surrounded by the richly dressed company, she stared after him, thoughtfully. Why were so many men his enemies? If he had faults, they numbered no more than others. In spite of much talk in his disfavour, she would always regard him with respect. His brother held the people's love, but who strove to rule while the King was away? Alys understood nothing of nations or warfare or intrigues in high places, but it seemed to her simple reasoning, that the King was needed in his own land, not fighting for some spot in the East however holy. Surely it was to this estate that God called him, and for that, he had been born. She shook her head a little to dismiss from her mind affairs of such high moment. There was enough at Birlstone to occupy her for the present, and she was glad that it should be so, for then she had no time to dwell on the sick empty feeling of loss that gnawed at her heart. Gilbert gave her a strange glance as she passed him. She frowned a little icily. The man had pressed over near, as though anxious to hear what passed between herself and her royal visitor. She had never altogether trusted the man, and now that there was no Sir Geoffrey to bring him to book, she was somewhat concerned at his manner. However, she decided to await developments.

She had not long to do so. A week later came a messenger from Sir William de Lacey. He was admitted to the bailey, accompanied by six men-at-arms. Alys frowned imperiously as he asked if she could read, and at her answer, proferred a letter. She broke the seal, and read the contents, written in a clerkly hand, hardly likely to have been penned by Sir William himself. Some shaveling clerk or chaplain had written obviously at his command. The message was peremptory, though masked in a courteous manner. It had come to his notice that his serf, Blanchette, was living at Birlstone, and he requested that the girl should be handed over to his officers. He felt sure that Lady Alys would be pleased to comply with his request.

Alys rolled up the parchment and gazed proudly back at the messenger.

"Sir William de Lacey is mistaken. Birlstone is no refuge for any one whom he can claim as his rightful property. Were it so, it would only be just, that I answer his demand."

"My Lady, Sir William has it on good authority that

the seamstress Blanchette, the daughter of his former steward Rolf, lives in your castle."

"Then he is rightly informed. Blanchette *is* my seamstress, but she is no bondswoman. Rolf was a freeman, a yeoman. Sir William has no claim to the person of his daughter."

The officer's horse moved impatiently, and he dragged at the bridle rein, savagely forcing the beast to a halt. "I am to infer that you refuse to give up the girl?" His voice was insolent.

"Sir William may infer what he pleases. I shall inform Blanchette of his wishes. If it is her desire to leave Birlstone and come to Mountsorrel, she may do so. I will send her with an escort. If she prefers to stay with me, I shall grant her my protection."

There was a little stir behind her. Alys's eyes caught those of Walter, who grunted in agreement. The six men-at-arms moved closer together as hostile glances were cast at them, and whispers rose in anger at the implied insult to their chatelaine.

The messenger's voice rolled over the courtyard, "You realise, Lady Alys, that Sir William is prepared to back up his demand with force."

Her voice did not falter. "Then we must be prepared to defend Birlstone. I will do so if necessary. Please convey my regrets to Sir William, now I suggest that you return at once."

The little knot of servants moved forward further to menace the riders from Mountsorrel and Alys ordered them back. Muttering they obeyed her, gathering in a group again, after the troop had clattered over the drawbridge. Walter signalled for it to be raised and came to her side.

"I am sorry, Walter," she said quietly, "but I cannot allow myself to tamely submit to the abduction of this girl. She has a right to seek shelter here."

"My Lady, it is not for me to question your decision. Clearly enough, our people are willing enough to support you, but this is what I feared. De Lacey knows that part of our force remains in Wales. He believes the garrison to be below strength, and uses this as an excuse to force entrance."

"I think you are right. How soon might we expect an attack?"

He shrugged, "Any time. I think it wiser to lower the portcullis and keep the drawbridge raised. I will order a careful watch on the battlements and inspect the arms. You need not fear the effects of a siege. Stores are more than adequate and there is water in plenty. I pray that de Lacey will prefer a waiting game, believing that you will be easily intimidated. Before long, we should expect reinforcements, when the men from Wales return."

"And if they do not come to our aid, soon?"

"Why, lady, then if it is your command, we will defend Birlstone to the last man. You are our lady and you carry our heir."

She forced a smile and placed one white hand on his leathern clad sleeve, "I know none of you will betray my trust. Report to me later and let me know what orders you think best to impose. What of the manor folk? Some are working within the castle. You intend to allow them to leave?"

"It would be expedient if some of the elderly and infirm sought shelter in the castle. De Lacey's men could attack the village in search of supplies. It is ever his way to allow them to plunder and loot."

For the first time she faltered. She had not thought what the consequences of her reply would have on her people. "I had not thought of their danger," she confessed, "we should send a warning to the village."

"Send Oswin, lady. He can be trusted well enough."

Oswin's face was grave when he faced her in the hall. "Lady," he burst out at last, "has it slipped your notice that some one in the castle informed de Lacey of Blanchette's presence here—someone you would be wise to watch?"

She lifted her head in surprise. "Until recently I imposed no rule of silence on the people. Rolf himself said he hears much gossip from the various taverns he frequents." Oswin was silent and she said sharply, "Whom do you accuse?"

"I accuse no one, lady. It would be ill to do so, since I have no proof, only I say to you beware Gilbert, that is all." Immediately he left on his errand, and she was left to ponder over his warning. It was not unexpected. True enough, as she had said, de Lacey might have gained his information from village talk, yet she doubted it. There was a tacit understanding she knew, between villagers and outlaws. No one would wittingly have given away the girl's presence. If Gilbert had betrayed her, it was well that Walter should be aware of her suspicions and she decided to inform him that evening when be reported to her.

Blanchette received the news without emotion. "Lady," she said quietly, "if it were best for me to go, I will leave Birlstone."

"I knew that would be your answer," Alys said firmly, "and since it is so, I shall keep you close. You shall be my prisoner. I promised your father I would keep you safe, and so you shall remain." With this Blanchette had to be content.

For the next four days the occupants of the castle lived in a state of uneasy watchfulness. No word was received from de Lacey, but Alys knew full well he would not remain content with her reply. In time the Prince would send instructions, but before that would be the time to attack. If he were determined to force Blanchette from Birlstone, now was the time to attempt it. She continued to wait in a state of dull hopelessness for a report from Wales, but it seemed that her husband's officials were in no hurry to keep her informed. Even one or two men-at-arms, experienced in siege craft, would be of use, in the defence of the castle. She knew Walter was concerned, though he said no word and continued to busy himself with watching their defences. Her face paled as she saw her men stolidly preparing vessels of lime and pitch, deadly weapons in use against possible invaders. Her woman's soul revolted against the idea of men screaming under a stream of molten lead or pitch, or falling blinded under a shower of lime. Yet she knew his preparations were necessary. She moved from keep to stables, battlements to bailey, heartening the men and watching their work. Elfrida chided her on overtiring herself, and reluctantly, she retired afterwards to try to rest in her room, but sleep evaded her and ever present was the dull continuing ache of her loss.

On the fifth day, Elfrida woke her to tell her Walter was calling for her. Alys sat up startled. It was hardly light, but Elfrida's frightened expression told her the matter was urgent. She reached for a furred robe to cover her nakedness and signed for the captain to be admitted.

"It has come, My Lady," he said quietly, "we are besieged."

Alys regarded him steadily. She wasted no time in begging him to contradict himself. He was the bearer of ill tidings, but be required her immediate attention.

"Have they begun the attack?"

"No, My Lady, so far no movement to begin. We can see them from the walls. They must have been marching all night bringing up the scaling ladders and tents for supplies. Three they have already erected. There is no sign of a battering ram nor heavy siege weapons but de Lacey has them at Mountsorrel. It is known."

She nodded. "He is very confident. Moving in the darkness he has brought up light equipment, hoping to scare me into surrender. To move up an arblast or trebuchet would excite comment and he counts on speed to bring us to our knees before the Prince can aid me."

"You think Prince John will do that, lady?" Walter's question was respectful but she looked at him sharply. He was not the only one to doubt the Prince's motives. She resolutely thrust aside the thought that he would leave her to her fate, since there was naught to be gained by coming to her assistance.

"He promised me aid," she said evenly, "the problem will be to reach him. I thought we should have more warning. I should have dispatched a messenger earlier, but since I had nothing of which to accuse de Lacey, it seemed bad policy."

"We will wait awhile, lady and see what ensues. I have called the garrison to the battlements. Will you dress and come to the hall? You must stay within the keep."

"That I shall not do."

"My Lady, you must think of your child."

"Walter, I never cease to think of it. It is for him I intend to hold Birlstone. Do not fear, old friend, I will not be foolish, I shall take your advice, but I must see for myself the dangers."

He smiled briefly, saluted her and withdrew. Blanchette assisted Elfrida to dress her and they ate a silent meal, hastily. Not even Elfrida scolded her, when she slipped a cloak round her shoulders and mounted to the battlements, for Walter to show her the enemy encamped. She could not have believed de Lacey to command so many men. Already the castle was cut off from the road, as two rough wooden palisades had been hastily erected to encircle it. She watched as further replacements moved up bringing the tall scaling ladders for the attack on the walls. Of de Lacey himself, there was no sign. The men scurried about like ants, assembling equipment at the bidding of their captains. Her own men waited stolidly on the battlements, acknowledging her presence with respectful nods.

"So many men, Walter. Surely these are not all garrisoned at Mountsorrel."

"No, lady, he must have employed mercenaries."

"Then he planned this months ago—all this to take back a girl he desires. There are dozens in the villages he could have without a fraction of this expense incurred."

"Lady, it is Birlstone de Lacey wants—nothing else."

Her eyes were troubled. "Have we a chance, Walter?"

"Against this equipment yes—against mining engineers and mangonels, no. We must hope for assistance in good time."

"Why does Guilbert linger in Wales? He must know he is needed here. His master's child needs his protection."

"Does he know about the child, lady?"

She turned startled, her hazel eyes wide. "No, since you mention it, he does not, but what keeps him in the Marches?"

"I know not, lady, but I pray he comes swiftly. It is likely that de Lacey will begin a war of nerves and delay his attack. He thinks you a weak woman, easily bullied into submission. He will try to play cat and mouse with you."

She forced a grim smile. "I pray you are right, Walter. If it is so, two can play at that game. He will learn that I am not easily intimidated."

It seemed Walter had guessed true, since no message or attack was made during the day. The besieging army contented itself in preventing anyone from leaving or entering the castle. Beyond that, it did nothing. The defenders spent a chilly Spring day on the battlements, their nerves strung to breaking point, their weapons at the ready. At intervals they relieved each other and as darkness descended, Walter reported no further progress.

"It is what I suspected," he said when making his report. "They hope to tire us before the attack. De Lacey must know we are short of able-bodied defenders. You yourself must rest, lady. This can go on for some time. Keep a good heart, the longer he delays, the better our chances. We have stores in plenty and could hold out against a siege for a year or longer."

The next two days proved nerve racking. The defenders were over anxious and aimed at all who drew near the walls to jeer upwards. Walter commanded them to hold their fire, since they merely wasted arrows, and those they must reserve at all costs. Alys found it difficult to sleep. She agreed to Elfrida's urging and lay on her bed, while either her nurse or Blanchette kept watch by her side, but in spite of her brave words, her fears grew, as the days passed. She had heard tales from her father of the pillage and rape which followed on the capture of a castle. Surely it would not come to that. Someone would come to her aid. She grew stern with herself. If she feared now, during the calm before the attack, how would she acquit herself when it came?

She was to discover soon. The three women were seated in the solar early on the fourth day, from the first sight of the besiegers, when they were silenced in their talk, by a roar from the bailey. Alys rose to her feet and held up her hand for quiet. Elfrida gave a frightened little moan and Blanchette came to her side and placed a comforting hand on hers.

"It has begun."

"I must go to the walls."

"No, My Lady," Elfrida scrambled to her feet, throwing out a hand to detain her. "We must stay here. Yonder is men's work."

"True, Elfrida, but since there is no master to hearten them, their mistress must suffice."

"But your child, Lady Alys . . ."

"Hush, Elfrida. I will be cautious. Remain here and heat some water in the entrance room. Call all the women together. We must prepare for the wounded."

She descended the keep stairs and met Walter returning from the bailey. "It has started, My Lady. They are moving their ladders into position. Do not fear, our men are driving them back."

"Have they siege weapons?"

"I think I spied a trebuchet, but they have made no effort to use it yet, nor has the battering ram been moved up. I think this but a ploy. Four of our archers are wounded, but not seriously."

"May I see?"

He hesitated, then nodded and led the way to a side walk of the battlements, instructing her to remain well back from the line of fire. She peered down at the scene of confusion and destruction below. Men running beneath fell back before the constant stream of arrows from the gate-house defenders. A sudden scream froze her blood as five of the attackers fell from their ladders under a flood of boiling oil, clutching their faces and arms. The ladder toppled and the men hurtled backwards to land on a knot of their retreating comrades. So far it appeared that the advantage lay wholly with the defenders, but she knew such a state of affairs could not continue to exist if heavy mining weapons were brought into play later. She turned from the walls and returned to the entrance hall to supervise the attention being given to the wounded. She bit her lip as the men cried out sharply, when comrades broke off the shafts and roughly abstracted the arrow heads. If only Ibrahim had been here to give his aid. Oswin looked up at her in passing. He was busily engaged in heating water. Even yet, Walter had forbidden him to use the weapon which Sir Geoffrey had denied him. She was surprised to see him, being under the impression that he had left the castle and returned to his mother's hut. In her pain, she had not thought to be relieved at the thought that Geoffrey's death had brought him release from the payment of the penalty decreed.

When evening came, the attackers drew off, but the occupants of the castle spent a restless night, many of them nursing their wounds. Alys did what she could to help, then went to assist other women to tear up linen for bandages and prepare oil and lime for the next day. At last, she returned to her apartment to spend a quiet hour at her prieu-dieu.

As the expected attack did not commence at first light, the defenders waited anxiously, dreading a new phase. As the watery sun rose above the gate-house, Walter called Alys to the battlements. He pointed down to where the familiar form of de Lacey's messenger had ridden close to the gate, under a flag of truce. The men-at-arms on the gate-house watched him warily. He stilled his rearing mount and called loudly on the still air.

"Sir William de Lacey regrets the necessity of this

course of action, lady. If you will grant his request, hand over the person of Blanchette and allow him free access to the castle, he will call off the attack, if not, he will send out his battering ram to crash down the gates."

"He will find it hard to do that. He must first fill up the ditch and he has no siege tower, nevertheless, in time our defenders will tire," Walter grumbled, his eyes tiredly scanning the enemy entrenchments.

"Ignore the challenge, Walter. Let the messenger return to his master unanswered," Alys said quietly and withdrew with him to the bailey. "Why oh why doesn't Alain Guilbert come? If I could only look to his coming and hearten the men, we could hold out."

Walter nodded and as he left her to drum up further enthusiasm among his wearied men, she stood for a moment watching the stable lads watering the horses. Their usually glossy coats had remained ungroomed during the last few days, since all but essential tasks had had to be abandoned. Oswin came up to her, anxious to reassure.

"Lady, do not fear. We will go on supporting you— till death if need be."

"Perhaps that is what I most fear, Oswin," she returned quietly. She was moving away when she called him to her again. "Your mother, you have not seen her for some days?"

"No, lady," he hesitated, and looked away. "I am concerned for her but I could not leave you."

"You know a way out of the castle?"

"Yes, lady—behind . . ."

"Tell me nothing. I ask only one question. If you went that way, what would be your chances of slipping through the cordon?"

He shrugged. "Not good, but I can try."

"Then go, Oswin. Tell no one. It may be that what you say is true. De Lacey knows more than he should, of what goes on in Birlstone. Reach Rolf and tell him of Blanchette's danger. Ask him to advise you how best to reach the ear of the Prince. I must have help, and quickly."

He nodded, stooped and kissed her fingers. "God guard you, lady."

"And you, Oswin. Take care."

She watched him go from her into the stables, and for a moment thought to recall him. She might be sending him to his death, yet could she guarantee the safety of anyone in Birlstone? Surely he had as much chance as any of them.

The attack was resumed within the hour and she found herself too occupied to worry about Oswin. She stayed within the keep at Walter's insistence but outside she could hear the noise of battle. By noon a new sound was heard above the shrieks and shouts of combat, a trundling of wheels. De Lacey was moving up his siege equipment. When Walter came to the hall to consume a hasty meal, he confirmed her surmise.

"They are attempting to fill in the ditch, to place the battering ram in position against the main gate. We have held them off so far, but there aren't enough men to keep them back. Tom and Roger were killed this morning and four more are wounded, two of them now unable to hold bows. He has brought an arblast into action and they are loading the trebuchet."

"Then we have little chance. If they breach the outer wall, we are defenceless."

"To do that, they must cross the dry moat. Take heart, remember each hour, they lose men too."

"I know it—so many dead and maimed. When will it end, Walter?"

"Lady, it is *how* it ends which concerns me."

Nothing was said of Oswin's disappearance. It was likely that it had not even been noted. Alys did not doubt that he had gone. He would do what she asked, whatever it cost him.

The women worked tirelessly through the day and night. Not even Elfrida voiced a protest, though her haggard eyes followed Alys as she moved about the keep. The entrance hall and upstairs niches had now been converted into an infirmary, where the men lay and moaned in their pain. Walter himself carried his left arm in an improvised sling. He had been struck by an iron javelin and the limb hung useless. He made no complaints, but Alys thought it gave him excruciating pain whenever he moved. Her eyes sought those of Blanchette over his head, while the girl was fashioning the linen sling to immobilise the arm, and she shook her head. She did not venture into the courtyard now since the heavy stones and lighted brands of pitch came hurtling across the walls at irregular intervals and she knew the men feared for her safety and felt easier in their minds, when she remained in the keep. Her only hope now lay in Rolf. She knew his small band could do little, but if he were able to alert the Prince, then he might send aid. For this she prayed constantly. She had lost count of the days. Doggedly she kept on with her tasks, only aware of keeping safe Birlstone for the child who was coming.

If Oswin's suspicions of Gilbert were correct, the man showed no sign of any pleasure in his betrayal. He was white to the lips and babbled in prayer as the wounded were carried into the keep. Prompted roughly by Walter, he attended to the stores and kept the scullions at their work of preparing food. Whenever possible, he avoided leaving the shelter of the keep, but commanded to the stables to see that the horses were fed and watered, since there was no one else to send, he went, though under protest. He came rushing back into the keep within minutes.

"Lady Alys," he shouted hoarsely, "Sir William himself is at the gate. The attack is halted. He requests talk with you."

Alys got up from her knees, where she had been giving water to a fevered archer. She was slow-witted with fatigue, "Sir William, you say?"

"Aye, lady. Walter advises you to ignore him, but I say you must listen to him or we shall all die."

Blanchette came to Alys's side. "Be quiet, cur, would you have her endanger herself?"

"She is endangering us, everyone of us, to keep you in safety."

"If I thought that, I would find a way to climb the wall this moment but . . ."

"Hush Blanchette. I must go out and listen to what he has to say."

"Lady, I beg of you . . ."

"Please, Blanchette, let me go." Both women were weak and tired, yet they struggled feebly, the one seeking to detain, the other, to free herself. Momentarily the stronger, Alys shook herself free and ran to the doorway, her progress aided by Gilbert who blocked Blanchette's way.

From the steps of the keep, she stared across the ruin of the courtyard. Walter called to her from the battlements.

"Back, lady. Let me deal with this."

She paused only for a second, then gathering her torn skirts in her hand, she ran down and into the open. Walter urgently waved her back but she stood still and called imperatively to him.

"Let me come up. I must hear what he wants."

"I can talk with him and relay the message."

Sir William's voice carried clearly over the sudden hush. "I will parley only with Lady Alys. Let her see me. I am unarmed. See, I remain in reach of your archers. Do you not trust me?"

Since she was determined, Walter signalled to an archer to assist her onto the battlement walk and drew her back behind the shelter of its crenellations.

"Very well, Sir William, talk. The Lady Alys hears you."

"You must surrender the castle. You have no choice. There is no aid forthcoming, you must know that by now. There is no hope. I have no wish to leave Birlstone in ruins."

"Then withdraw your men and leave us in peace, Sir." Her voice was clear, tired, but it did not falter.

"You know I will not do that, until you meet my terms. Allow me free entry and we will talk."

"That I will not do. I hold Birlstone in trust for my husband's heirs."

"Then they may keep naught *but* Birlstone. If you refuse my offer, I shall fire the village."

Alys caught her breath in sudden fear. "You cannot mean what you say. The villagers are no threat to your security."

"Defy me, and you shall see the Church flames lighten the evening sky." He turned and rode back towards his men. Alys watched him, her hand tightening on the wall. She was caught, like a stag with its back to the wall, when it turns at bay to face the hunt. There was no way out. She could not allow the Church and the manor huts to be destroyed. He had used the one weapon against which she was powerless.

"Open the gate, Walter," she said quietly, "Let Sir William enter."

"No, I beg you, Lady Alys, do not do that." She turned to see Blanchette crossing the courtyard. "Let me down to them. I and I alone, am what he says he desires, his only pretext for the attack. Walter can let me down by rope. Do not open the gate."

"Go back, Blanchette. I have no intention of delivering you to Sir William. Go back into the keep. I intend only to parley. His greed is well known, perhaps he will take ransom."

"You cannot risk the lives of your people." Blanchette had started across the bailey, though Alys waved her back. Walter turned, his attention diverted by sounds of resuming conflict. The men on the battlements were all looking towards the enemy, their hearts touched with the cold chill of fear for dependants in the village. They were all unprepared for the boulder which came hurtling over the wall, slung from the trebuchet, which had recommenced firing, after the failure of the truce. Alys screamed a warning, then covered her face with her hand to shut out the sight of Blanchette's slight crumpled form on the dirt floor of the bailey, which was already sticky with the girl's life blood. She tore down the steps and sank to the ground, lifting the golden head onto her knee. Already the lovely eyes were glazing, but she was still able to speak though with effort.

"Do not grieve, Lady Alys. Do not trust de Lacey even when he offers fair terms. He is unable to keep faith—it is not in him—he is rotten to the core . . . as my mother found to her cost."

"Blanchette, I have no choice, the manor will burn. He means what he says."

The girl was no longer capable of reasoned thought. She clutched blindly upwards for Alys's hand. "My father," she whispered, "let him not seek revenge. Tell him I died by accident. It was so. Already his life is seared by hate . . . no more . . . there must be no more . . ."

"I promise." Alys bent forward to kiss the chilled brow, so lovely even in death.

"Bear Sir Geoffrey a son . . ."

The last words were accompanied by a tired smile and Alys stared down dry eyed at the body of the girl who had been her first and only confidante. Mechanically she bent forward and closed the eyelids then gently straightened the crumpled limbs. She forced herself to repeat the act of contrition, and the prayer for the dead. Like so many of them Blanchette had died unshriven, but Alys had no fears for her. She was unaware of the sounds of renewed combat, until she looked up into Walter's tired eyes.

"Open the gates I said, Walter. Let Sir William take what he desires."

He bent down and assisted her to rise, then without argument he commanded that the portcullis should be raised and the drawbridge lowered.

She stood by his side, a straight proud figure as de Lacey rode across the drawbridge and dismounted, signalling his men to remain in the castle entrance. He stared at her white, set face and the dark stains marring her kirtle.

"Take Blanchette, Sir William. She lies there. She is yours."

His eyes flickered to the crumpled form, then he expelled a sigh of distress. His grey eyes were troubled.

"Will you believe me, Lady Alys, when I say I had no wish that this should happen."

"Whether I believe or disbelieve, it is immaterial," her tone was flat, unemotional. "Now what do you want—whatever it is, take it and go."

He had recovered himself almost immediately and averted his eyes from the still form. "You require protection, Lady Alys," he said suavely.

Her tone was bitter. "Protection, Sir William, from whom and what, would you say I needed protection?"

A slight smile crept to his eyes. "You are wearied, lady. You cannot remain here. I suggest you accompany me to Mountsorrel where you can rest undisturbed."

She turned and looked full at him, her hazel eyes direct and showing utter contempt. Despite himself, he lowered his own and turned to his men who awaited his orders.

"Bring up a litter. Lady Alys rides with us."

Walter placed a hand on her shoulder, but she removed it gently and shook her head.

"Sir William, you swear to me that my men here and the manor folk will remain unmolested."

"I swear it on the Holy Rood."

"Then I will go with you. I may take my woman?"

"Certainly, and all you require for your comfort. There is no hurry. We will await your pleasure."

She walked from him into the keep entrance and Elfrida gathered her into her arms.

"Will you come with me, Elfrida? It must be your own choice, none shall force you."

"Can you doubt me, lady?"

"Then come, we must not keep our jailors waiting." She passed in from his sight. He stood. unmoved by her insulting reference to his own role, then turned to his captain to give further orders.

Three hours later, Lady Alys de Courcelles left Birlstone riding in a litter escorted by sixty of William de Lacey's picked men-at-arms. What able-bodied men who were left at Birlstone, were rounded up and taken as prisoners, the rest injured and dispirited were left to lick their wounds, and seek their relations in the village.

Chapter Eleven

OSWIN WEARILY pulled his shaggy pony to a halt and rubbed his eyes to make quite certain they were not deceiving him. There, at the head of the pass, he could see the grey massive outlines of Gwyndd Castle. He had arrived at last after five weeks of journeying. He would make the last stage before night fell and he must reach his destination before the drawbridge was raised. He urged his unwilling pony to a last effort, and pressed on with dogged determination.

Even now he could not forget the sight of the courtyard at Birlstone when he had entered with Rolf that fatal day. Even before they crossed the drawbridge, they knew they had come too late. Already the mercenary army had left and debris littered the countryside round Birlstone. Rolf had tightened his lips and rode on, his little knot of followers more cautiously remaining at the rear. Walter had greeted them. He was superintending arrangements for the burial.

Rolf crossed to where his daughter lay and uncovered her face, free now from the dark blanket with which Walter had himself covered her. He touched her bright hair caressingly just once, then he nodded to the men who had come to lift her slight form and bear her away. Oswin had stood beside him while they laid her in the earth, not expecting words and unable to offer any of comfort. His heart yearned to know of Lady Alys, but sorrowed for the bright, gay girl who had gone.

Afterwards Walter had briefly explained the situation. The castle was now virtually unguarded. Only the sick, old, and wounded had been left behind. He himself was weak with exhaustion and strain and clearly must rest before attempting any further course of action. Quietly, Oswin had waited for the outlaw to advise him. He did so competently. There would be time to mourn later. Now was the time to act.

"Oswin, you must ride to Gwyndd and inform Alain Guilbert, Sir Geoffrey's squire, what has happened here. No one here is fit to go and I am unacceptable as a messenger. When Walter is somewhat recovered, he must ride to Nottingham and send word to the Prince. It is poor hope, but the best we can make. Since Lady Alys carries Sir Geoffrey's child, Alain Guilbert must claim the castle in his name, or if a daughter, she will become in her turn, a ward of court and is entitled to crown protection. I will keep watch near here and do what I can to aid the villagers if they are attacked."

"Lady Alys, he will not harm her?"

"I think not. De Lacey wants only Birlstone. I am surprised he has not manned it, but doubtless he thinks it unnecessary at the present time."

"But how *can* he claim Birlstone?"

"He holds the person of Lady Alys and the unborn heir."

"Then . . ."

"If I know de Lacey, he will aspire to marry the widow. In this, we must thwart him, if we can. Are there horses in the stables?"

"Aye," Walter nodded wearily, "but they've been sore neglected of late. I'll have the best saddled for Oswin. 'Tis lucky he rides."

"Then I'll give directions for the way." One of the servants fed Oswin and tied up some bread and cheese in a kerchief. While he ate, he listened to Rolf, then rising, prepared to leave. There were three hours of

daylight yet and he would not waste them. Walter
spoke authoritatively as he entered the kitchen.

"You'll ride armed, lad?"

Oswin hesitated. He touched the hunting knife at his
belt, then held out his hands for the bow and quiver
Walter proffered.

It had been a difficult journey for a boy who had
never been further from home than his own village.
Walter had furnished him with a little money and he
had been able to buy food at small hostelries on the
way. At night he had preferred to sleep under hedgerows, bitter cold though it had been on occasions,
rather than trust himself to some of the villainous looking owners of inns. Once he had been questioned by
the men of the sheriff, but had given satisfactory answers and had been given leave to proceed. During the
later stages, he had several times mistaken his way, and
now that he was in the Marches, he found the inhabitants strange and was unable to understand their
tongue. His horse had gone lame two days ago, but after a bitter exchange with an innkeeper in Chester, he
had exchanged him for the slow but sturdy animal he
was now bestriding. Now at last, he was in sight of his
goal. He prayed that Sir Geoffrey's squire would recognise him, and listen to his tale.

The portcullis had been lowered when he arrived at
the gate, though the drawbridge had not yet been
raised. Darkness had not quite descended, but Gwyndd
had been subject to frequent raids from the fierce
Welsh supporters of the Prince Llewelyn, and the
castle inhabitants kept careful watch over its defences.
Oswin was relieved to see the familiar gryphon device
on the guard's tunic, when he was roughly challenged.

"Oswin, a serf from Sir Geoffrey's manor at
Birlstone. I bring tidings from Lady Alys de Courcelles
to his squire, Alain Guilbert. The matter is urgent."

The man looked him over, then nodded and allowed
him entrance. He rode under the portcullis which was
raised at a given signal and into the courtyard. The
castle seemed orderly enough. Oswin's throat tightened

as he saw men going about the familiar tasks which had been his own at Birlstone. He swayed when he dismounted, for he had gone without food that day, unable to find a native of the area able to understand his requests. The steward, a thin, tall, precise, individual, listened to his explanation and was at first inclined to consider him of little importance, but as the boy insisted on word with Alain Guilbert, he signalled for him to accompany him into the keep, fastidiously keeping his distance from the mud encrusted figure.

He was escorted to a largish room opening off from the great hall and bidden to wait in the doorway. After some moments, the steward returned and signalled to him to enter. He paused and looked round eagerly for the man he sought. Alain Guilbert was a young dandy of a knight, much given to embellishment and ornament. Nevertheless he was known to be an intrepid fighter and held the respect of the men. Oswin swallowed a sigh of relief as he saw him rise from a heavy wooden chair near the bed and come out of the shadows to receive him.

"Lord, you will perhaps not know me, Oswin, one of the serfs from Birlstone."

A familiar cool voice from the shadows arrested him in his tracks and made him question the validity of his own senses.

"Come into the light, Oswin. I would see you more clearly."

It was impossible. Oswin placed a hand to his head. He was overcome with exhaustion. That voice could not be what he thought, but the foppish squire gestured him forward towards a high bed, and he caught one of the bed-posts to support him. Owsin knew that voice too well to be mistaken. Had it not on more than one occasion dealt out punishment? It was weak, but true enough. He stared wonderingly at the man who was reclining against the pillows. It was growing dark in the room but he could just make out the mass of fair hair, and unfamiliar reddish tinted beard, but the cold, direct blue eyes were unmistakable. Instinctively,

Oswin's hand moved to the bow over his shoulder, the
weapon the man in the bed had forbidden him ever to
grasp again, on pain of death. He slipped to one knee
and breathed a prayer of heartfelt gratitude.

"Sir Geoffrey. God be priased. I thought to never
hear you speak again. We had thought you dead."

"Near enough," the voice sounded faintly amused,
"but what is it, lad, you are in no state to stand on ceremony. The Lady Alys, she is well?"

"Sir, you have not heard? By all the saints, I pray
you, send at once. Sir William de Lacey has attacked
Birlstone and taken Lady Alys to his castle at Mountsorrel. You must go instantly, Sir. She carries your
child under her heart."

One thin, blue-veined hand tightened on the coverlet
and there were gasps from the group round the bed.
Now Oswin was able to see the Saracen physician was
in attendance, and he moved forward, anxious to check
any hasty decision to be made by the sick man.

"So." Sir Geoffrey's voice was cold. "So that is what
brings you to Wales. The castle garrison?"

"Fought bravely for many days, Sir, hoping for aid
from Master Alain here. Then de Lacey threatened to
burn the village and Lady Alys surrendered herself, believing you to be killed in a foray, and none to aid
her."

"I see. You have done well to reach me. I see you
came well armed." A slight smile curved the bearded
lips. "As you see I have been incapacitated of late. For
almost two months I have lain immobile with a lance
thrust in my left thigh. Thanks be to God, I am almost
whole again."

"Sir Geoffrey, I must remind you, you are still unfit
to sit in the saddle." The Saracen's alien tone was respectful but authoritative.

"Then what is to be done, Ibrahim?" the question
was faintly mocking. "Do you propose I lie here, while
my lady rots at Mountsorrel?"

"No, of course not. I cannot prevent you, but I
counsel you to ride the first part of the way in a litter."

For a moment Oswin thought the baron would argue, but after one direct glance at his adviser, he nodded, but pushed back the covering. "You are right, old friend, of course, but I must try my wings and walk to supper in the hall. Alain, order our departure for first light. If I must travel slowly like a woman, at least let us make an early start. As for you, lad, my steward shall convey you first to the kitchen and then to a mattress, where you must rest well, if you are to go with us tomorrow."

The cavalcade progressed more swiftly than Oswin could have imagined, since they were well horsed and knew their way. Even so, it was almost three weeks before they came in sight of Nottingham, for in spite of his ardent desire for speed, Sir Geoffrey's weakness forced him to stop by the way. At Chester he had been unable to rise from his bed for three days since an attempt to ride had brought on heavy bleeding from his thigh wound and Ibrahim threatened to tie him down if he disobeyed him. Seething with frustrated fury, the baron was impelled to give way. He lay back in the only bed the inn boasted and insisted that Oswin should remain at his side and give him a minute to minute account of what had occurred.

"So she mounted the battlements to parley? So, and she was well when you last saw her, big with child you say?"

"Aye, Sir. Your child should be born before Easter, and my lady so happy. Before she heard . . ." he broke off then pressed on, "before the troubles, she used to sing while she worked at the tapestry. It did the heart good to hear her. She was tired and worried at the last, but quite well. Walter said she seemed calm enough when she left. Please God, but he could not harm her. You do not believe that, Sir Geoffrey?"

"No, lad. She will be safe enough from de Lacey. She is the heiress to Birlstone but . . ." He bit his lips, "I pray God protects her from danger. The horrors she has witnessed may have brought on a miscarriage and endangered her life. I did not know of the child."

Oswin looked up at him puzzled and he frowned. "She did not choose to inform me. She must have known well enough. Doubtless she had her reasons." He looked at the boy oddly then smiled. "And in the attack you used the weapon I know you to be proficient with?"

"No, Lord," Oswin kept his eyes on the floor. "Walter forbade it. I carried it to Gwyndd since he said I must be armed. I have since surrendered it."

"H'm, perhaps that was unwise. You may yet have need of it."

In spite of Sir Geoffrey's frustration, it was clear that the enforced delay did him good service. By the time they neared Nottingham, he was in the saddle, and seemed near to his old self again, though Ibrahim urged him to rest whenever possible. At the castle, they learned that the Prince was in Winchester. Messages had been sent informing him of de Lacey's felonious attack on Birlstone. So far, no reply had been received. The castle castellan gazed thoughtfully at Sir Geoffrey's well armed force and pursed his lips. He seemed about to comment but, looking up into the grim face above him, he appeared to change his mind. The baron gave orders to take the road for Mountsorrel.

Five miles from the turning which would take them in view of the castle, they were halted by a fallen log which blocked the road. The captain-at-arms swore and ordered the obstruction removed, but Sir Geoffrey, hearing a rustling above them, checked him with a wave of his hand. He waited until the man he expected stepped from a thicket and surveyed him fearlessly, his eyes sizing up the armed force and returning steadily to its leader.

"Well met, Rolf," Sir Geoffrey said quietly, "I expected you."

"I cannot say the same but even so, you are welcome. Will you and your men accompany me, sir. I would speak with you."

Sir Geoffrey glanced back then nodded and Alain Guilbert gave the order to dismount and lead the horses into the wood. Almost at once, they found themselves surrounded by silent forms which appeared to rise up from the ground or step from the tree trunks themselves, to serve as their guides. Sir Geoffrey gave his stallion into the care of Oswin, and followed the outlaw leader to his retreat. He sat down on a felled log and drank gratefully from a leathern jack of ale. The other waited, and he said as he placed it down by his feet, "I grieve for you, Rolf. It was hard to lose Blanchette. Do not fear. De Lacey shall pay."

"Aye," the other gave a grim smile, "of that I have no doubt, but it is the living who concern me at the moment. You intend to demand your lady's release and back up your demand with armed force?"

"Certainly."

The other sat down opposite. "I do not counsel it. He will kill her."

"He dare not."

"Nevertheless he will do so. I know the man."

The baron's face was suddenly grey from anxiety and fatigue. "Dammit, man, what do you suggest I do? Wait until the Prince orders her release?"

"It might be wiser. When John learns you survived, he will be forced to command her release. This will be a shock to him. Like all of us, he believed you dead. I did not recognise you myself at first, the beard disguises your features. De Lacey thinks himself secure from your vengeance at least."

"Then surely *now* is the time to strike."

"It may take days to force an entrance. In that time Lady Alys will be lost to you. His women never survive his interest. It is his way. At present, he guards her well, thinking he may well become her husband. If he discovers the futility of his hopes, he will destroy her."

"I dare not wait for the Prince to move. The man has much to occupy his mind, too much to move to crush one rebellious subject, however he might wish to do so." Sir Geoffrey rose to stretch his cramped limbs and move across the grass. Interestedly Rolf watched his altered gait. "The Lady Alys will soon bear my child. She must be got clear of Mountsorrel as soon as is possible."

"Very true. You mistake me, my lord. I do not counsel you to wait, only to caution."

The baron checked his pacing and stared hard at the outlaw. "You have thought of a plan?"

"Not exactly, but this I know, Lady Alys must be clear of the castle before your force attacks the gate. Someone must enter and effect her escape."

The blue eyes gleamed appreciatively. "Shrewd reasoning, friend. We must think how best it can be done. Does de Lacey keep strict guard?"

The other shrugged. "He expects no sudden reprisals. He knows of course that Alain Guilbert is likely to present himself before the gate, but he reckons on the fact that he holds the most powerful hostage, to protect him at present. No, the village folk enter as usual and with them the odd pedlar, vegetable seller, an entertainer or two. He keeps court at the castle. It comes to my mind that we need to send in a message by one the Lady Alys would recognise and trust." He paused. "Unfortunately, not myself. De Lacey knows me too well, though I can furnish whoever enters with details of the layout of the keep, guard house and courtyards. No—I thought perhaps the boy Oswin might be an admirable choice, if he will take the risk." He looked across to Oswin who stood some way off, anxiously watching their discussion. At the outlaw's signal he came at once, eager to offer assistance.

"No, Oswin cannot go alone. I will not countenance it. I must know how she is, if she is fit to make the escape. If any enter, it must be me." He waited for Rolf to argue, but the man was silent. He looked across to one of his men, who was restringing his lute.

"Do you sing?" he questioned, in what seemed an irrelevant change of tone.

The baron raised his head and stared at him. "Sometimes," he said, "in my youth, I learned to strum the lute and sing foolish troubadour love poems. We all do it." He followed Rolf's gaze, and a smile crept to his blue eyes. "It is possible," he nodded, "I was said to have some skill, though active service has robbed me of the desire for such praise. Here, fellow, let me try your instrument."

The man complied at once and the baron took the lute and strummed experimentally, then broke into a not unpleasing baritone rendering of a ballad popular in Brittany, some four or five years ago.

Alain Guilbert listened, then as the last note died, he said, "The notion is fraught with risks, Sir."

"You are not complimentary, Alain," the baron laughed as the younger man frowned.

"Nay, Sir, I am no critic. Your voice seems pleasing enough to me, but you may easily be recognised. De Lacey knows you. Do you forget he was your antagonist in the lists and only recently?"

"But he thinks me dead."

"True," Rolf leaned forward and stared into the baron's face. "The element of surprise lessens the risk. Your hair is longer and the beard hides that firm chin. I think it likely, he would be deceived. Even Lady Alys will not easily suspect. We must remember she could easily give away the intruder more out of shock than of any willingness to betray. She too thinks you dead."

Sir Geoffrey looked coldly at his squire. "There are risks, Alain, no one denies it, but they have to be taken. Rolf speaks true. We must be sure of Lady Alys's safety before we dare to attack. You will lie hidden with Rolf, near to Mountsorrel, until you receive a signal from me to begin. In the meantime, I will assure myself of my lady's condition before planning any way of escape. If necessary," his voice hardened, "I can kill de Lacey, though it might not guarantee her safety. You agree?"

"I will do what you command, Sir, though I am concerned for your safety. Will you not let me accompany you?"

"No, you must lead the attack. No, if the lad will take the risk, I shall take Oswin. He is the obvious choice. He can go as my servant. He loves Lady Alys."

"Sir, I pray you let me serve you," Oswin dropped to one knee, his eyes beseeching.

"You know the danger?"

"Aye, Sir."

Sir Geoffrey touched his shoulder in a comforting grip. "I have cause to know how you love her. You will not fail her in this. Now, Rolf, since you say you know the buildings well, I trust you have some plan to effect an escape. I shall trust to your judgement. Can you help us?"

"I think so. Come into the hut, Sir. My men will serve you food. I have drawn a plan as accurately as I remember. There is one way and one way only from the keep, while the portcullis is down, as it will of necessity be—but come, I will explain."

〰️ *Chapter Twelve*

ALYS WAVED Elfrida away with an irritated gesture, as she approached with her jewel box. There could be no point in drawing attention to her appearance at this time. She would have much preferred to eat in her apartment, but that Sir William, ever deliberately courteous, had insisted. She wondered what line he would take if she decided to openly oppose him. Would the silky soft tone turn to one of harsh command? Possibly not, but he would see that she obeyed him. Tonight as always, she must go down to the great hall and suffer his company. Immediately contrite, she turned to Elfrida.

"I'm sorry, Elfrida. Forgive me. I am edgy for no reason."

"You have good enough reason, lady." The older

woman placed a comforting hand on her sleeve. "You are feeling tired and dispirited, but it will soon be over. You will soon hold your child in your arms."

Alys stared bleakly at her reflection in the mirror her woman held. It was a fine one of glass brought from the East, unlike anything she had owned. "Would it could be at Birlstone," she whispered and closed her eyes to hide, even from her nurse, her naked fear.

"Soon enough that too. The Prince will send you aid. He must."

"Why must he, Elfrida? I am a weak woman. What can it matter to him if I am forced to marry a man I hate?"

"He has declared himself then?"

"Not yet. At present he is all polite condolence, constantly murmuring sympathetic phrases to comfort me in my loss, but I know full well his determination is to acquire Birlstone and to do that, he must marry me."

"What will you do?"

"I don't know, Elfrida. I simply don't know. I shall refuse, but I can see no way of avoiding it in the end. I was so determined before, not to marry Geoffrey de Courcelles. Finally I was forced to do so, for the good of my people."

"But this will not please the manor folk."

"It is not the villagers' security I am concerned about."

"The child?"

"Yes—my child. That is all that matters to me now. It is all I have left. Come, we must go down. Stay as close to me as possible."

"Lady, I will."

Despite her promise, Elfrida was separated from her mistress during the meal by the length of the great trestle table. Above the salt sat Sir William de Lacey with Lady Alys on his right, and with them at the high table were his chaplain, a measly mean-spirited man called Friar Roger, his steward and captain-at-arms, a burly bull of a creature whose manners were more fitted to the stables than a noble's household. Alys picked nervously at her food, while de Lacey watched her sardonically over the rim of his goblet. He was richly dressed as usual this evening, and she could not deny he made a brave figure, in dull yellow, his curling auburn locks falling onto his shoulders in studied disarray. As they had done often, her eyes strayed to the gold chain which had been her husband's Christmas gift which de Lacey now wore as an ornament with its irregular piece of amber setting off the yellow of his surcoat, against which it glowed darkly. She never saw him without it. The bauble seemed a talisman. She longed to demand its return, for his insolent flaunting of her property angered and disturbed her but she knew he would reply with some flowery evasion, so she averted her gaze.

At the close of the meal, he stood up and drew back her chair. "It is more pleasant in the solar," he said. His words were an invitation, but his tone implied command. She glanced back once towards Elfrida, then allowed herself to be led away. The little private apartment, off the hall, was indeed very pleasant and comfortable, almost luxurious. Eastern rugs and one silky animal skin strewed the floor, and tapestries kept out the draughts. De Lacey escorted her to a carved seat and offered her wine from Burgundy. She accepted the goblet, though toyed with the wine, having always been abstemious by upbringing and the liquid was potent. He stood before her, toying with the piece of amber, and she flushed under his scrutiny.

"Now we are private, Sir William," she said embarrassment making her voice sharp, "I will ask you again when it will please you to allow me to return to Birlstone?"

He smiled, took his time before answering, and seated himself. "I am grieved that you scorn my poor hospitality, Lady Alys," he said evenly. "I had hoped to have pleased you."

"You have treated me at all times with courtesy. Nevertheless I wish to return to my own place, and speedily."

"The Prince would never forgive me if I allowed you to remain unprotected at Birlstone, and in so delicate a condition," he murmured quietly.

"That, Sir, is stronger reason. I would wish Sir Geoffrey's heir to be born in his own manor of Birlstone."

His grey eyes gleamed oddly. "I assure you, my dear, I think only of your welfare. I have procured for you the services of the finest midwife in Nottingham. She will be here within the next few days. Your safety is my primary concern."

A cold finger of fear touched Alys's heart. She could not have said why. She looked at him directly and his mouth continued to smile, but the eyes were cold. De Lacey was anxious for her safety, but what of the child? She thrust away the thought that he would not wish any heir to survive. Throughout the weeks of captivity he had held himself aloof, made no attempts to court her, it seemed she was merely the welcome guest at Mountsorrel, but she could not forgo a shiver of distaste when he came near her. A strange disquiet never left her. Somehow she must escape from his house and before the birth of her child. Her tortured mind had gone over every possibility. She had lain nightly in a cold sweat of panic, but there seemed no way out. She was alone, but for Elfrida, who was well-meaning but helpless to aid her. Her apartment was well guarded, though the presence of her jailors was never allowed to intrude on her privacy. The gate house was well defended. Escape seemed impossible. De Lacey allowed her no access to outsiders. She held no talk with the villagers, and even the castle servants were watched when they served her. Only Elfrida was allowed to remain alone with her mistress. So far she had envisaged no plan to send even a plea for help to the outside world. Now even the woman who was to attend her in childbed was his chosen creature. She strove to make her voice normal.

"I have said before, Sir, I can see no reason for your concern. Why should I need protection at my own castle of Birlstone?"

"You forget you are a wealthy widow, there will be suitors in plenty."

"And you intend to be the first and only one in the field."

He smiled again broadly. "I have never attempted to conceal my admiration."

She stood up clumsily and knocked over the goblet on the table by her side. Angrily, she dabbed at the spilt wine with her napkin and he took it from her hands and soaked up the excess. Her hands were trembling.

"Are you all the same? Geoffrey de Courcelles wanted me only that he might seize Birlstone. Were it not my child's only inheritance, I would yield it to you today, that I might be free of it—and of you."

"Only inheritance? You jest, Lady Alys."

She turned back to him. "I misunderstand you, Sir. My meaning is clear enough."

"Do you not know that your child will be one of the wealthiest heirs of England? De Courcelles want Birlstone? Whyever should he want so small a manor, when he has a castle in the Welsh Marches, land in Hampshire and estates in Brittany three times the size of any holdings in England?"

She sat down abruptly, and stared at him unbelievingly. "You tell me that it was not for the manor that de Courcelles asked for my hand—or was it that he did not do so, was it the Prince's command?"

He came to her side, throwing aside the wine-stained napkin. "I find it strange that you are unaware of the facts. Certainly de Courcelles asked for your hand. Many poor knights who were anxious to win you were angry enough at the time. I myself was among their number. We wondered how much he offered to line John's pocket, but learned later, he was a favoured friend of the King, whom he met on crusade, and indeed of John himself, for whom he appears to hold some respect. For the life of me I have never been able to determine why."

Alys knew her question to appear stupid yet could

not forbear to ask it. "But why should he want me, *me* of all people, if as you say, the castle is nothing to him, merely an encumbrance?"

De Lacey shrugged expressively. "I know not. He had seen you, it appears, some time before the death of your father."

"But I had never left Birlstone, except on one occasion when I visited Nottingham, with my father, but my stay was very brief, merely three or four days."

"But he *did* see you, reason enough. I confess at the time I had not done so and my only interest stemmed from my need to acquire Birlstone."

"Do not mock me, Sir. Make no pretty speeches. You want Birlstone. Do not pretend you desire me too."

He leaned over her chair-arm and took her hand. She attempted to free herself but he held it firmly.

"I do not deny that were you penniless, I would not seek your hand. I tell you frankly, I could not afford to do so. Whatever my faults, I have ever been honest. I have never concealed from any woman my intentions but, Alys, you must believe what I tell you now, whatever you think of me. If you will take me as your husband I *swear* you will not regret your act. I will cherish you and hold you safe. True I had never set eyes on you until that day in the wood, equally true I coveted your land, but from that time, I was the victim—you the enslaver, see," he touched the amber on his breast. "This stone symbolises in part my love for you. When I took it, I planned to use it to discomfit your husband, I confess it. He had taken what I wanted and I planned that he should smart for it. I did not think he would ride in the mêlée. Later, when I stared at it, I knew why he had chosen it for you. It has a quality of golden beauty which you possess, in it. If you look closely, you will see some insect entrapped." He gave a short laugh. "I thought never to see William de Lacey in such thraldom. I am that fly, Lady Alys—no, do not turn away your head, believe me in this. You are like no woman I have ever met—a nut brown maid in truth and one of steel. I have loved many women. The word has been over-used on my lips so much that now when I want most to use it, it seems glib on my tongue, too slight to mean what I wish. You think yourself the prisoner here, but know this, I stand in grave peril if the Prince command me to yield you up, yet I will defy him if I must. De Lacey has ever put his own concerns first and considered his own skin, but not in this."

She drew back, in spite of herself, half convinced by the sincerity of his tone, which had for once dropped its suave politeness. "If you feel for me as you say, you will release me and allow me free choice," she said challengingly.

He stood upright and shook his head, his mouth once more a little bitter. "No, Alys de Courcelles. What I have, I hold, and I hold you. John may command me, and I shall be for a while under the weight of his displeasure but he will not strive to force me. He has other business. John angles for England while his brother is away. Do you think he will halt his plans to aid the plight of one woman, however wealthy? Come now, be sensible. I shall not press you. Your time of mourning is hardly begun. In the meantime, remain my honoured guest and think well on what I have said. Wed me of your own free will, and you will not want for anything, least of all the love of your husband." His manner changed again and he was once more the solicitous host. "You are tired. Rest in your apartment. To-morrow you will see the problem differently. You are a sensible, brave girl. I think perhaps it is those traits I most admire in you. You will see the wisdom of giving way gracefully. I will call your woman."

When Elfrida had left her, Alys tossed and turned on her bed. Her nurse slept close by, separated from her only by a curtain. She knew the woman to be concerned about her and could not rise, as she would have wished, to pace the chamber. She sat up and strove to consider her thoughts. Two questions revolved in her brain. Why had Geoffrey de Courcelles married her if not for the land, for what reason? He had not loved her. Had he wed her for pity? Her face flamed at the thought. Distasteful as the truth was, it had to be faced. She felt she could have borne anything but that. The second doubt was yet more deadly. Her child she now knew to be heir to a considerable estate. Would de Lacey allow that frail life to lie between him and what he coveted? Until the birth, she was safe. He would do nothing to endanger her safe deliverance, but afterwards, what then? She caught her breath at the enormity of her unspoken accusation. Now, more than ever, she knew she must escape, but as de Lacey had made no attempt to hide from her his designs, she would be more carefully guarded than previously. Her brain ached with the effort to devise some way out but it was useless. When the first streaks of dawn touched the slitted window of her chamber, she fell back on her pillows, exhausted with the futility of desperation, and slept like one dead.

Elfrida expressed concern in the morning at the dark shadows under her eyes. She watched anxiously. It was still almost three weeks before the child was due, but the girl had gone through so much during the later months of pregnancy, that anything might happen. Wisely, she made no comment and asked no questions. As Alys had risen late, a servant brought them bread, meat and ale to the apartment, and she sat listlessly picking at the food. When he returned afterwards to collect the tray and empty vessels, he seemed inclined to chatter. He appeared new to castle service. Elfrida could not recollect having seen him before. He was obviously a country lad with a broad open countenance and a shock of untidy yellow hair. Sir William, he told them, had returned from hunting with a companion, he had met at the inn, The Green Man. The stranger was a foreigner, a Breton, so they said, very elegant and soft spoken with a strange accent, which made the serving wenches giggle. He was handsome too, they said, with long curling fair hair and a pointed beard. He sat now with Sir William, drinking by the fire in the hall, for it had come on to rain. The sky was leaden.

There would be no more riding out today. They had expressed a desire to play chess later. The man had been accompanied by his servant, an English boy, who had joined them in the kitchen. Alys showed little interest. Sir William's drinking companions were no concern of hers, but Elfrida was inclined to lend an ear to his gossip.

"You say he is a stranger to these parts."

"Aye, Lady. He has been all round the country, they say, recently in the Welsh Marches."

Alys lifted her head curiously at this intelligence, but the boy's next pronouncement vanquished her interest.

"His servant says he is a troubadour, not a professional musician, you understand, but a Nobleman—younger son of a Breton Count. He collects songs for pleasure and has come to England to listen to our minstrels and return to his own land with new ballads. For this reason he has been much travelled."

As the boy clattered away, Elfrida expressed curiosity. "If the man is a stranger, it is odd that Sir William invited him here."

"True, but he has himself been little better than a prisoner these last weeks. If the man has travelled, he can relate court gossip, and he may sing later, to entertain Sir William."

"What an occupation for a nobleman's son."

"In France they have many such interests. I heard that in Provence they hold courts of love to discuss amorous behaviour and promote gallant conduct in the art of courtship. To sing love poems to your lady is considered a knightly accomplishment, not effeminate as we would suppose it here."

"Could he carry a message for you, lady? It might be possible."

"It is unlikely that I shall be allowed private talk with him, even so, I could hardly trust such a man with a plea for assistance. Elfrida, I sent such a plea, but I have been ignored. I shall not seek to see this man. I am in no shape for displaying my person in company."

When Sir William requested that she join them in

the hall, she begged to be excused and requested food
served in her apartment. Sir William complied, and she
was thankful not to have to engage in conversation
during the meal. From the hall she heard a gust of
laughter, punctuated by the sound of tankards banging
on the trestles. Doubtless the man had proved an engaging companion. She was about to retire, when the
man-at-arms entered her apartment unceremonially
and lounged insolently in the doorway.

"Sir William requests you join us. His visitor, Pierre
de St. Rivieux has been persuaded to sing. Sir William
thinks it will divert you."

"I have no desire to be diverted, Sirrah. I am tired.
Please leave me."

"Nevertheless, I think you will come, lady. The man
has been told of you and desires to meet you."

"Indeed," Alys fumed at the man's insolence, won-
dering how de Lacey had explained her presence in the
castle. Did the knightly troubadour consider her some
light of love? She was half inclined to press her refusal,
then too tired to argue, gave way and coldly informed
the man, she would join him with her maid, in several
moments. Determined to put on a brave front, she allowed Elfrida to apply a little salve to her lips and pale
cheeks, and at length, entered the hall.

She did not glance in the stranger's direction, as Sir
William came forward to greet her. Under her lashes,
she noticed that he had risen to his feet courteously.
She seated herself at Sir William's insistence.

"I felt you must partake of the pleasure. Pierre de
St. Rivieux is about to play for us. Music is his abiding
interest. He is most honoured to meet you."

Alys inclined her head somewhat frostily. She half
glanced at the man before accepting the goblet of wine
from de Lacey's hands. He was as the boy had said, an
elegant creature, rather slight, though quite tall and
fair. He was dressed in a mantle of blue velvet which
became his fairness and ruddy tinted beard. He bowed
to her gracefully, one hand holding his lute, which was
embellished with trailing ribbons of many colours. His

voice was foreign, pleasantly accented, with the slightest hint of a lisp.

"Sir William does me much honour in allowing me the privilege of meeting you, lady. I am grieved to hear of your loss."

"You are kind, Sir."

"You would permit me to sing for you?"

"I would be delighted."

"Some love song perhaps, a sad ballad of unrequited love, or a poem in praise of beauty. I am at your command, fair lady."

"No—no. I am in no humour for tales of love. Sing me of some brave deed, some hero, anything you choose."

"With pleasure, lady." He touched the strings once or twice and smiled across at Sir William, who nodded to him, while signalling to a servant to bring more wine. He had drunk deep during the afternoon and was already in a mellow mood. He strolled across to the far side of the hall, to breathe the cold air and clear the wine fumes.

The Breton began to sing to his own accompaniment. His voice was a pleasing baritone, clear and true. Alys found herself relaxing under the power of the music. He had chosen a heroic tale, taken from the old Icelandic saga of a voyage to the lands of the West. She was intrigued by the story of suffering and endurance, fears that faced those intrepid explorers of unchartered seas, their longings for home and family, the loves that they left behind. The voice gained in power as he described a mighty storm, which arose and almost swamped their vessel, and sank to a caressing note when relating the triumphant return of the heroes and their reception by those who had mourned them as dead.

She was smiling as the last chord sounded and he turned, eager for her criticism.

"Bravely sung, Sir Knight. It was an unusual choice. I have not heard a minstrel sing such a song, but my father kept little company, and few visited us at Birlstone."

"It has been my delight to revel in the strange tales I have gathered in my journeyings. I intend to write them down on my return to my estates, that other men may use the collection. Let me sing you one of my latest acquisitions, a translation from the Welsh. The people of the Marches speak a strange outlandish tongue, but their music is from heaven. Listen, here is a love song."

She placed her fingers across the goblet and shook her head as Sir William advanced with a flagon of wine. He grinned and moved away, pouring himself another goblet. He had enjoyed the heroic tale, though one of battle might have proved more interesting, but the love poems, he considered effeminate, moon struck. He threw himself into a chair, and stretched out his long legs, and allowed himself the solace of more wine. Lady Alys had no eyes for him this evening. He half regretted his impulse in inviting this elegant stranger, yet the man had a ready wit, and had amused him earlier with his biting comments on court society, and his bawdy tales. He yawned, the room was overwarm and the wine potent. Jesus, his throat was dry. The food had been palatable and well spiced. He needed yet more wine to wash it down. He lovingly surveyed the flagon and reached again to refill his cup.

Alys's eyes had filled with tears at the beauty of the song. The Breton did not await permission before beginning again. His voice dropped to a low note and he rose and moved nearer to her, aware now that he had her full attention. Before, she had not been really curious about his appearance. Now, as he approached, she looked full at him, forgetful of her former embarrassment about her obvious condition of late pregnancy. She had been mistaken if she had thought his features womanly. The long hair and beard had misled her. There was firmness in the set of the chin and in the candid blue eyes. She stared up at those eyes hypnotised; wide spaced, direct, utterly commanding. She caught her breath abruptly and thoroughly alarmed, half rose. He did not falter in his singing, but raised one sardonic eyebrow, questioning her movement. Alys felt sudden blackness hovering round her consciousness. She could not believe what she thought she had seen. She put out one hand towards him, whether to halt his advance or draw him nearer to herself, she could not have told, then she slumped forward, a dead weight into his arms. De Lacey half rose as the singer's voice was hastily cut off and the lute fell to the floor with a discordant jangle of chords.

"Do not alarm yourself, Sir William. The lady has but swooned. I fear it is the heat of the room. She is not well."

"By all the saints—it is not yet her time, but one is never sure. I will call her maid."

"Nay, let me take her to her own place. I think she needs only to rest. She had excused herself earlier, I recall, and we over-persuaded her to come to the hall."

"True." Sir William swayed a little on his feet. He was feeling somewhat confused and hardly knew what was best to be done. Before he could protest further, the Breton had ordered a servant to precede him to Lady Alys's apartment, and he himself bore her in the man's wake.

Elfrida hovered around thoroughly alarmed, but he laid her down on the bed and gestured to her to draw across the tapestry and send away the curious servant.

"It is nothing. Bring some rose water and let me bathe her temples. She is coming to."

Alys came out of her swoon to stare up into his face. He placed one quick hand on her mouth and spoke.

"Quiet now. Do not be afraid. I am mortal. It is not what you fear."

"Geoffrey . . ." the word was whispered, almost a sigh.

He nodded very gently, then spoke more loudly.

"See, lady, you are better. I am grieved to have disturbed you. In my desire to sing for you, I demanded your company when you were unwell. Please forgive me."

"It is nothing, Sir Knight. It was but a momentary swoon. I am often now a little faint."

His mouth was very close to her ear. "I will come to you later. Do not undress. Be prepared. You understand?" She nodded as he bathed her temples and gave the pad to Elfrida, and moved away.

Sir William de Lacey had thrust aside the tapestry and stood, frowning down at them. Alys pushed herself up on her pillows and forced a smile.

"I am sorry, Sir William. I was dizzy. I had not been well earlier, you remember. I am better now."

"You are sure?" He peered down at her doubtfully, but was reassured by the conviction in her voice.

"Quite sure. Please leave me to rest. I need only Elfrida."

The Breton shook his head, smiling, and together they left. Alys sat, listening to de Lacey's half stumbling footsteps, then she fell back on the pillows, bottom lip caught in her sharp teeth.

Elfrida leaned towards her. "My Lady, you have no pains?"

"No, no, Elfrida, none I tell you," she looked up warningly. "You must be careful. All is well."

"But that man . . ."

"Was Sir Geoffrey."

Elfrida's eyes opened wide at Alys's whisper.

"I know it is hard to believe—but it is so. Silent now. You heard him. We must wait until later, but be ready."

Alys turned from her attendant, and stared up at the window. Even though she had spoken with conviction, she could hardly believe it herself. It was indeed Geoffrey. She had seen him, heard him—but how? She told herself that she was delirious. It was impossible. She had prayed for aid, and she but imagined that it had come to her in a guise so wonderful. Yet it was so. She would not lose faith. He had said he would come, and she would prepare for him. As the evening wore on, she pretended to sleep. Her back ached and her heart was beating fast. Excitement was making her restless, yet she must lie patiently, until he declared himself. She knew Elfrida too was restless behind her dividing curtain, and knew the woman's fears were more for her condition, than a belated hope that rescue was at hand. The sounds of the castle at last began to die down. The noise of feasting had long been over, and all she heard now was the sound of straw rustling from the hall as the household serfs disposed themselves to slumber. Through the slit at the side of the arras, she could see that the brands in the hall were burning low.

When he put back the tapestry, she sat up at once, soundlessly. She could only see him dimly as he groped his way to her side.

"Are you dressed?"

She pushed back the covers and stood up. "I am quite ready but for my shoes."

"Rouse Elfrida. It were better if *you* do it. She may cry out if I touch her."

She nodded and moving the dividing curtain aside, bent over her nurse. Elfrida roused immediately and made no outcry. She too was dressed and joined them quietly. She stared bemused at Sir Geoffrey, who shook his head gently, enjoining silence, then gestured them to sit on the bed.

"You are sure you are fit to go with me. It will not be easy. You are not like to . . . ?"

She cut him short. "I am quite ready. I have said it, there are two weeks yet. I swooned from shock of seeing you."

Elfrida's whisper was high pitched. "My Lady, you cannot go. You will have to climb—the child!"

"I *must*, Elfrida," low as Aly's answer was, it was commanding. "If I stay here, de Lacey will kill my child. He cannot acquire my lands without so doing and if Sir Geoffrey's presence is discovered here, he will kill him too. Take a hold on yourself."

"My Lady . . ." the woman's answer was tearful and Sir Geoffrey spoke quietly. "If you are afraid,

Elfrida, it were better if you remain here. Sir William de Lacey wishes you no harm. My men will attack by sun-rise, but you should be in no danger if you remain within the keep. Lady Alys must go *before* the attack you understand?"

"Yes, Sir."

"Good, now listen for I have little time. Tear off the skirt of your robe, for as Elfrida says, you must climb. Trust me, and you will be safe. Put on a warm cloak for the night is chill. The men are snoring in the hall. They have drunk well. We must pass by them, so stay close to me. There should be enough light to see. If one stirs, do not fear, he will think you are a drinking companion on the way to the privy or some woman seeking her lover. We go down the keep-stairs to the kitchens. I will then tell you what to do."

She stood up at once, without question. Tears were pouring down Elfrida's face, as she embraced her. Even so, she cried quietly. Sir Geoffrey took his wife's arm and led her to the curtained opening. He stood for a second listening, then impelled her forward. Alys knew the castle better indeed than he did. She made no difficulties at following him into the hall. The brands were burning very low now. One or two were merely issuing black smoke. All around, men were drawn up in attitudes of sleep, breathing heavily. Sir William de Lacey slept in a private apartment on the other side of the chapel, but his captain-at-arms was stirring restlessly. He had fallen forward onto the trestle table, one hand dabbled in spilt wine. She paused at sight of him, then seeing her husband's beckoning gesture, hurried on. The far end of the hall was deep in shadow and she drew back startled as she almost fell over a sprawled body near the door. A sleepy groom roused himself angrily, cursed the clumsy one and settled himself down again. The door was open, fortunately, and Sir Geoffrey drew her onto the keep-stairs. Again he paused, staring into the black well of the stairway. He knew well enough that de Lacey would not sleep without being well guarded, but he had kept his eyes open

during the day and gauged the times when the archers
were like to pass certain points. There was risk certainly but men-at-arms were creatures of habit and
they had little to fear on such a night. Their lord was
even tempered, having drunk himself to slumber. They
were more afraid that de Lacey would catch them
slacking, than of any possibility of attack. Since both
their captain and lord were easy in their minds, they
would do only the minimum duty required of them. In
this lay his hope of success. He touched her arm and
pointed downstairs.

Alys pattered in his wake. He was as sure-footed as
a cat but she stumbled once or twice in the dark, and
he ran back to steady her. Cold sweat stood out on her
brow and she thought what harm a fall down the stone
steps could do. She pulled herself together and felt
gingerly for each foothold. Safety must come before
speed. If she fell, she would destroy them all.

At the bottom, he drew her sharply right into the
entrance room and kitchens. The great door was
barred and he made no attempt to try it. It would be
defended from the outside, and was not his goal. From
behind the wooden butcher's chopping block, a dark
form rose to confront them, and Alys caught back a
scream.

"Oswin?" Sir Geoffrey's voice was authoritative.

"Aye, Sir." She caught the boy's hands and he
squeezed them hard.

"Oh, Oswin—I thought never to see you again."

"Is the way clear?" Sir Geoffrey cut urgently across
her greeting.

"Aye, Sir. The cook sleeps in that alcove. He is dead
to the world. He needed no tempting from me to drink
deep. The scullions went to the hall."

"We passed them. Stand firm in case that fool cook
wakes. Come to the window, Alys."

She obeyed at once and stared upwards at one window which seemed larger than the other arrow slits. Sir
Geoffrey quietly drew forward a wooden stool and
drawing his hunting knife, mounted. Rolf had told him

of this one large window on the ground floor. Some years ago FitzParnel had stayed in residence. He had brought with him his own cook, a finnicky fellow from Normandy who had complained bitterly of the dimness of the kitchen. To pacify the man, whose rich dishes he enjoyed, FitzParnel had had the window enlarged, and since the embrasure let in cold winds in winter, the window had been covered with thin horn. Sir Geoffrey tried his knife experimentally and grunted his relief when it struck through the opaque substance somewhat easily. Oswin stayed watchful behind them in case his erstwhile drinking companion roused from his noisy slumber. Pale light streamed through the aperture as he lowered the horn to Oswin who slipped it quietly to the ground.

"I'll go through first, Oswin, and be ready to receive Lady Alys on the far side. Listen well. The window is a tight squeeze. Pull yourself through sideways and twist your shoulder. You will be able to see me do it. Sit on the window as I do, then twist and draw through your legs. It is not a big drop and in any case, I shall catch you. You are not afraid?" he asked as she peered upwards doubtfully.

She swallowed. Alys had never climbed in her life, since awkwardness in childhood had prevented such escapades, but she nodded. The pain in her back was increasing, but she would be well enough when they were clear of the keep. Oswin placed a comforting hand on her shoulder, as she anxiously watched her husband wriggle his way through. Though he seemed thinner than the last time they had met, he was a big man, and she thought for a moment, he would not make it. He swore softly then was through, and dropped lightly to the ground. He stood up and glanced hurriedly round. They were in shadow. The moon was not up but he could see the burly figure of the guard on the gatehouse across the bailey. He whispered urgently back to them.

"Right Oswin—now. It will be simple enough for you. Help Lady Alys all you can from your end." Alys shook off his hand and mounted the stool. She had watched carefully and obeyed him. It was not as difficult as she had thought. She slipped her shoulders through and gazed down. Her husband stood below, a solid black shape in the darkness then she drew her legs upwards and sat outwards looking into the dark bailey. He reached upwards and she slipped awkwardly downwards into his arms. It took only a moment for the more agile Oswin to join them. Now she saw that he had bound his bow carefully against his shoulder, and he stooped to loosen a rope wound tightly round his waist, under his homespun tunic.

"I have the rope, Sir," he said quietly.

"Good. We make for the battlements, there," he stabbed the darkness with a deliberate finger. We shall have to tackle one of the guards. He will make a cry almost certainly, but it is unlikely to be noted if we are swift. You know what to do, Oswin."

The boy made no reply and Geoffrey took Alys's hand to lead her round the angle of the keep to face the battlements. He was alarmed to find her huddled against the wall.

"What is it? Did you twist yourself in the climb?"

"No—no I am well enough. I get breathless easily. I am heavy with child, but quite unharmed."

"Then we make a run for it. I do not want the fellow on the gatehouse to catch sight of us. It is likely he has a horn and could wake the castle. I will go first with Lady Alys. Join us near the steps."

Again Oswin was silent, but she knew he noted his instructions. He had looped the rope over his other shoulder and was watching the gate tower. She found the run exhausting and was glad when Geoffrey bade her crouch down under the battlements' steps, until Oswin ran lightly up. They drew back into the shadows waiting, and Sir Geoffrey touched her lips in warning. Round the walk came the burly form of an archer. He was in no hurry, but paced steadily, looking outwards across the dry ditch towards the forestland beyond. Just once, he paused to locate his companion on the gatehouse and it was then that Sir Geoffrey sprang. Alys pushed a fist into her mouth as Oswin left her. She could hear heavy panting, the sound of scuffling feet, an inarticulate cry sounded loud enough in her ears, then silence. She leaned forward doubled up with a sudden sharp pain, then straightened as her husband's hand guided her up the steps on to the battlements. She thrust pity aside, as he drew her by a huddled form before their path.

Oswin was busy with the rope. He was making one end of it fast to one of the crenellations and leaning downwards to whistle softly to one who stood below.

"Now, my brave girl, you must do the hardest thing of all. You must slide down the rope. It will tear the flesh of your hands and not be comfortable, but it is not a steep drop and Rolf waits below to receive you. You can do it?"

She nodded tremulously and stared upwards at his dim features. Already she had become used to the grey light, but she could not make out his expression clearly.

"You are going first?"

"No—I do not go with you."

She caught at his arm but he shook her gently. "Trust me now. I know what I do. Rolf will carry you safely to sanctuary in Rothley. I have work to do here. Oswin goes with you."

She did not need to ask if he would return to danger. It would have been pointless and she was no stupid clinging woman to unman him when he most needed his wits and confidence.

"You cross your ankles so, round the rope. Rolf holds it firm below—then slither downwards. Do not look down. The ditch is dry though the ground uneven. Do not be afraid."

"I am not afraid," her voice was steady though whispered. "God go with you, My Lord."

"And with you." He lifted her and placed her on the wall then lowered her downwards and placed her legs on the rope.

"Steady now—hold on to me for one moment. When I let go, get a firm grip of the rope and let yourself go."

"One question, please answer me, though I know the time is inconvenient."

"There is time."

"Why did you marry me, Geoffrey de Courcelles?"

His answer was incredulous. "Why did I marry you—because I wanted you, of course—now go. Rolf is ready." She found herself slipping and strove to obey his instructions. Excruciating pain tore at her hands, then she found firm hands grip her body and Rolf lifted her clear and called up quickly to the two above.

She sat down on the grass while he gazed upwards. There seemed some delay. Sir Geoffrey had whispered one clear instruction to his serf.

"The watchman on the gate. Can you drop him from here?"

"I think so, Sir."

"Do your best, lad. I trust your marksmanship. If he cries out, I care not now."

Oswin drew his bow and frowned in concentration. The man's back in the grey light was a clear target. The arrow twanged through the air. The man made one startled cough and fell forward on to the crenellation of the battlements.

"Well aimed, lad. I wonder if you have disobeyed me and stayed in practice. Now over you go. You know what you have to do then."

"Aye, Sir—St. George protect you."

"He will, lad. He has always done so. Look to your lady."

Oswin descended the rope easily and Alys looked upwards just once as it came snaking down to fall at their feet. Rolf stooped and picked it up, raising one hand in salute. The dark figure drew back from the wall and Rolf drew her across the uneven ground to the shelter of the trees beyond.

Once in the wood, he stepped behind a broad oak

tree and drew forth a strange object which let out the glow of coals.

From his quiver, Oswin drew out an arrow and held one end deep in the brazier. Then he drew it forth and carefully placing it into the bow, sent it soaring high in the air. Alys stared upwards at its blazing path, smoke pouring behind like the tail of a comet.

"Sir Geoffrey's signal to his men," he explained quietly. "They wait to launch the attack and are reinforced by a party of the Prince's men who arrived at Birlstone yesterday."

Alys sent out a silent prayer to the Virgin. The gentle mother of God was all she could think of now. She only, could grant her aid.

"Rolf," she said huskily, "you must aid me. I am in labour. Can you get me to Rothley?"

He stooped and stared into her pale face, holding up the brazier to examine her more closely.

"Lass—that is too far," he said gently, "but never fear. We will keep you safe. Take the brazier, Oswin. I will take Lady Alys."

She bit her teeth down hard as he lifted her into his sturdy arms and set off at a steady pace through the trees.

Chapter Thirteen

ROLF LAID Alys down gently on the bed of bracken in his hut. The pains were coming faster now and he could see heavy drops of sweat on her brow. She made no outcries, but she was breathing heavily and small blood spots stained her lower lip, where she had bitten it hard.

"Now, lady," he aid gently, "try to relax. You will be safe here."

She smiled up at him. "You look more frightened than I, Rolf," she chided.

"Nay, lady, I will not leave you. I wish I could offer you a softer bed and the services of some woman."

"You have never played midwife then?"

"Not to a woman," he grinned down at her. "If need be, I will do what needs to be done, but rest easy, it may not come to that."

He left her for a moment, and went outside. He was more concerned than he liked to admit. There were no women in the little community, and Rothley was too far away to summon aid. He feared that the climb and hurried movements of the escape might have complicated the birth. If harm should come to her . . . He thrust the thought aside and turned to face the anxious gaze of Oswin.

"She is in pain?"

"Yes, lad. Do not fear. It is ever so—you have seen it often enough with the farm creatures."

"But surely it is before her time. Will the child come soon?"

"Unless I am much mistaken, yes. Oswin, take one of the horses and ride to Alain Guilbert's camp. Find Ibrahim and tell him his lady has need of him."

"You will stay with her?"

"Aye, lad." Oswin awaited no further prompting, but dashed off in search of a mount. Rolf hesitated for a moment then called one of his men and dispatched him in search of heated water, linen and fresh bracken, then he re-entered the hut. She greeted him bravely, but her fingers were clutching the dried fronds at her side. He brought over a home-spun blanket and put back her hair, now wet with sweat, with a weather-roughened, but gentle hand.

"How goes it with you, lady?"

"Well enough. It will take time. I have watched many hours with my mother. I am not inexperienced."

"Yet you are the only child."

"They all died. It was a great disappointment to my father. I must not do that to Sir Geoffrey."

"You will not fail him, lady." He looked up as a frightened boy entered with an earthen pitcher of warm water. He indicated for him to bring it over and curtly ordered the boy outside. She laughed again. "Everyone seems afraid of this but me—strange is it not?"

"Perhaps it is because we feel so helpless to aid you. I have sent for one more competent. Oswin has gone for Ibrahim."

"You should not have done that—the men may have need of him."

"And so have I, lady," he smiled again as she swallowed, and caught back a cry, "as you say, I am a coward."

"They will capture Mountsorrel." It was strange how confident she was. He marvelled that at the moment, she appeared to have no fears for Sir Geoffrey. Indeed, she had not. Her whole being was concentrated on giving him now a living child, a son if possible. She had made a bargain with him, and naught should keep her from fulfilling her part of it. Her frail weak mother had been so unhappy, and had earned only the contempt of her husband. Alys was determined that Geoffrey should have no such cause for complaint. Concern for his safety would come later. Now only the child mattered.

When Ibrahim arrived, she smiled at him gratefully. Rolf rose to his feet, relief apparent on his honest face. The physician took her slender wrist in his brown fingers, and placed a cool hand on her brow. "You may leave her with me now, friend," he said quietly.

When Alys heard her child's first cry, she was almost too exhausted to call anxiously to Ibrahim. He had turned away for a moment to examine the baby but returned almost at once to her side. He placed the new-born child briefly in her arms wrapped in a piece of clean linen.

"A son, Lady Alys. You can rest now."

She touched the tiny form with one weak hand and

gave a little sigh of contentment. It was finished. She allowed him to take up the child once more to bathe and dress him, and sank back on the pillows. Since there was no woman to assist him, Ibrahim cleansed the child, satisfied himself about its well being, and bound it in swaddling bands in Eastern fashion. He was gentle as a woman with Alys and she felt no trace of embarrassment at his skilled attentions. It was growing dark in the hut when she lay back with the child in the crook of her arm. He came over to her and sat down on a rough-hewn stool.

"You must be tired, Ibrahim."

"And you, lady."

She turned back the home-spun blanket and peered down into her son's wrinkled face. He was quiet now after the first lusty cries and she smiled at the closed lids fringed with pale golden lashes. Already she could detect some resemblance to his father.

"If I were sure of Geoffrey's safety, my happiness would be complete."

For the first time doubts assailed her. Now her travail was over, there was time to think of her husband's peril. Ibrahim reassured her.

"His force will overcome the garrison. They were reinforced by a party of the Prince's own retainers."

"John did send aid. I feared he would not." A warm note crept into her voice.

"The Prince has troubles in plenty. There is news that the King is on his way home and the nobles are ready enough to accuse him of mis-management of home affairs. There is much dissension among these Normans barons."

"Do you think there is truth in their assertions?"

He shrugged. "Perhaps—who knows? The barons like not a strong ruler. It suits them to regard John as a tyrant." He was eager to keep her mind from anxious thoughts about her husband's attack on Mountsorrel, and he was now himself expecting some news of progress.

"Ibrahim, tell me of Sir Geoffrey's injury—you know I believed him dead."

He nodded, "Oswin so informed us. It was unfortunate. Sir Geoffrey received a dangerous thigh wound while leading a sortie from Gwyndd against Welsh supporters of the Prince Llewelyn. The main force was drawn back and he became separated from his men. The Welsh took many prisoners, but left him for dead. The passes are desolate, especially in winter and early Spring and when he recovered enough to crawl, the rebels had ridden off. He forced himself to move, for to lie invited death in the freezing cold. Apparently a poor shepherd discovered him quite by accident, while searching for a lost sheep. He assisted him to his hut, where I believe he lay for days between life and death, semi-conscious.

"We at the castle had given him up as lost and it must have been this news which leaked back to the Prince and eventually reached you. At length Geoffrey recovered enough to write a message. He carried on his person a book of hours and tore a page from the manuscript, since his rescuer spoke no English. The man made his way to Gwyndd and I myself went back with him to succour Geoffrey. He was weak from loss of blood and I feared he would lose a limb, since the wound had festered, but St. George had defended him well, and he had not even suffered frost-bite during that terrible crawl. What agony he had endured during those two or three days (he could not say how long) I shall never know. We conveyed him many days later to the castle, where despite his protests I kept him to his bed."

"He has grown much thinner."

"True—and his cheek was badly grazed. For this reason he rejected the services of the barber and let his hair and beard grow. You must have been at a loss to recognise him."

"No," she said softly. "I would never have difficulty about that—once I had really looked at him."

He made no comment but sat quietly watching her

in the pale light which came from the door. For a space they remained still. He was unwilling to disturb her by rising and going in search of a lighted brand or taper. He hoped she would sleep a little but she stirred at length and he bent forward to listen.

"Does Rolf know about the baby?"

"He is not here. After I had washed the child, I went outside for a moment. I found Oswin sitting on the ground, anxiously waiting. I informed him that all was well, but he said Rolf had gone off shortly after I arrived. Oswin thought he had some problem concerning his men to deal with. Since I have heard no sounds of return, I imagine he is still away."

"He was good to me."

"Yes."

"You think Sir Geoffrey will be satisfied—that it is a son."

"Of course, though on the journey from Wales, he spoke of his delight should it be a daughter."

"Will you leave me to tell him?"

"If that is what you wish."

She smiled in the darkness and he rose now, since she was fully awake and groped around the hut till he found tinder box and tapers and lit up the poor shelter with a flickering glow, which at least allowed him sight of his patient. The child stirred in her arms and she held him closer. Reassured by her nearness, he fell into slumber once more, then abruptly the silence was broken by the sounds of men's voices and horses. She pushed herself weakly up and he stooped and built up the pillows under head and shoulders with some fur covering which had lain across another stool. Her eyes mutely appealed to him to investigate. Was it Rolf returning? Had he news of the attack? Ibrahim was about to step outside, when a tall shadow darkened the doorway, and Sir Geoffrey de Courcelles advanced further till he came within light of the tapers and stood near the make-shift bed. He looked just once at Ibrahim who nodded.

"All is well, Sir. I leave you with your lady." He

passed outside and Alys stared up at her husband. He seemed unhurt but for a gash, hastily bandaged on his right arm. She could see the blood-stain but it did not appear to incommode him. Dirt and filth marred his blue overtunic, and she exclaimed at the sight.

"You fought without armour?"

"I could hardly take mail into Mountsorrel with me. There was no time to acquire it later, never mind me. I am well enough. What of you?"

She undid the firm wrapping round the child and held him out for Sir Geoffrey to see. He wiped sweaty palm on his hose and bent forward to look.

"A son, Sir Geoffrey. I have fulfilled my part of our bargain. Will you keep yours?"

He was bemused at the sight of the child. Disturbed by the noise outside, it had opened violet-blue eyes to peer myopically upwards, but it yawned delicately and disposed itself once more to sleep. He smiled tenderly, but made no move to take the child from her.

"And you, my lady wife?"

"I am well, tired but happy."

He moved to the door and called to the boy outside. Oswin entered and stood wonderingly. For hours he had squatted outside waiting until she was delivered and Ibrahim had assured him of her safety. Now he was alarmed, disturbed by the summons. Sir Geoffrey had returned to her side, and he beckoned the boy impatiently forward.

"Come here, Oswin. Hold out your hands." The boy obeyed him wonderingly. "You will remember I threatened to take your hands if you disobeyed me?" Oswin flushed darkly and bowed his head. "However, there was a bargain made between Lady Alys and myself concerning these hands. Take my son into your arms."

Alys surrendered the child and he stood a little awkwardly, holding the unaccustomed burden close.

"I make you a present of your hands. Lady Alys has paid me the price for them, but you have earned more. You shall be free yeoman, Oswin, and when we return to Birlstone, I will make you a grant of land, but I ask you now to swear, while you hold him in your hands, that you will serve my son as long as you live, as faithfully as you have served his mother."

Tears welled in Oswin's eyes which he could not control or wipe away, since he continued to hold the child.

"You need not to ask, Sir Geoffrey," he said huskily, "nor do I need or want my freedom. All I wish is to serve you both. You know how I love her and will worship her child."

"Yet you shall have it. You solemnly swear."

"On the body of God—I swear."

"Give him back to his mother and leave us."

Alys took her son back into her arms and the boy went from them. Sir Geoffrey pulled forward the stool and sank wearily down on it.

"The siege goes well?" It was a statement rather than a question. She had complete faith in his ability to take Mountsorrel.

"Mountsorrel is ours. I opened the gate and lowered the drawbridge after Oswin killed the guard. They were completely unprepared and the Prince's men made us a formidable force. It was soon over."

"And de Lacey?"

"Dead." His blue eyes stared at her directly and she lowered her lashes, then closed her eyes and murmured a silent prayer.

"You feel pity for him?" She looked up at the odd note in his voice.

"He was not in a state of grace. He is deserving of our pity."

"Yet he would have killed you or the child and threatened to burn the church."

"Yes, even so."

"You surprise me," his tone was curt.

"He was a strange man. I could not understand him. I think I never shall."

"I did not fail to do so. His motives were clear enough—to take you and Birlstone." She was silent and he smiled a little grimly. "Perhaps you think it is an accusation you might level at me."

"That would be impossible, since I know you to be one of the wealthiest men in England."

"I have some authority."

"I find you just as difficult to understand."

"Indeed," in the taper glow she saw his fair brows arch upwards in the familiar expression of incredulity. "I have not considered myself a devious man."

"Why should you want me?"

"You asked me that before and I told you. I wanted you. It was as simple as that."

"But why, I am not beautiful and you had no need of Birlstone."

"Birlstone is not so inconsiderable. The manor is pleasing. My son will always love it, I think, since he was born here and it is his mother's gift to him. As to your beauty, I was not the only man to want you, as well you know."

"De Lacey wanted me only for my wealth. He believed I would inherit much of your property and desired to hold it. That was why I knew I must leave Mountsorrel before my child was born. He would have found some way to kill it, though I knew I was in labour, yet I could not delay."

He frowned. "You knew you were in labour when you went with me."

"I was not sure, but I feared it."

"Little fool. You should not have taken such a risk."

"Nor should you, when you stayed alone within the castle."

The frown relaxed. "There was no one else. To storm the gate might have taken days, even weeks, nevertheless we were talking of you. Yes, I believe he would have killed our child, yet I think he truly loved you, in spite of all." He took from the ornamental purse at his hips, a gold chain on which gleamed an irregular chunk of amber. She reached up with one free hand and took it from him.

"He was wearing it when he died?"

"He begged me to take it from his neck and return it. He said you would understand."

"I think I do—a little. How did he die, Geoffrey, was he wounded?"

"No." Again she detected that odd note in his voice and turned hurriedly to scrutinise his features.

"You did not kill him yourself?"

"No," he took her hand and stroked it gently. "I would have wished to do so. No, he fought bravely enough but I was never close enough in combat. One of my men disarmed him, and knowing my force to be in possession of the keep, he surrendered. He was unarmed."

"Then I do not understand . . ."

"I would have hanged him then and there on the battlements. I had the right and the Prince's captain would have borne witness to my just act. His life was forfeit and he knew it. He faced me squarely across the courtyard, but I had no choice."

"He did not hang then?"

"No, he was shot through the heart by an unknown marksman."

She drew a quick breath. "Rolf?" she whispered and he shrugged.

"I do not know. I do not *want* to know. He was here with you?"

Alys hesitated. She recalled Ibrahim's words. "He is not here. Oswin believes him to be dealing with some problem concerning his men." She shuddered slightly and clutched her child more closely. Once again she saw the bailey at Birlstone, and Blanchette's huddled form, her bright hair trailing in the dust. "He was with me most of the time I think. At first he stayed with me until Ibrahim came—then—then he waited outside."

He watched her carefully, then dropped his eyes. "It is well. It could not have been Rolf, some stray archer perhaps, the man had many enemies. It might even have been one of his own men. They had no cause to love him."

She remained silent. They would not speak of this

again. If Rolf had slain de Lacey, they both knew he had just cause. In any case, it mattered little. As if he read her thoughts, he said quietly, "I think he was glad it came so. He slipped to his knees and then he called me. I sent away the men and called for a priest, but it was too quick. The marksman had struck true. He died within moments. I had not even to withdraw the arrow. It was then he spoke of you and the girdle. He loved you, Alys. I am sure of that."

She fingered the amber. "In some strange way, I believe he did. He said he was caught like a fly. I am sorry, Geoffrey, that your gift should have come between us. At the time it meant much to me. It was the first jewel I ever received. You must believe me when I say I gave him no encouragement, and indeed I met him only the once."

"I know it."

"Why should he love me?" her whispered words reached him as he rose.

"Why indeed?" he said wryly.

At the door he turned. "I will leave you to rest now. It will be some days before we can move you to Birlstone."

"No. I am quite well. I will soon recover now. A night's sleep and I shall be fit enough to ride in a litter. You need not delay for me."

"By the way, Elfrida is outside. I will send her in. She was quite unhurt but half crazed with anxiety."

"Poor Elfrida. She will be unhappy she was not with me."

"Indeed she will. She had no idea you were so near your time."

"Had I told her, she would have tried to prevent me from going."

"Indeed had *I* known, you would not have gone," he retorted, a gleam appearing momentarily in his blue eyes, "but I will say no more, since you appear to have taken no hurt." He paused, then said thoughtfully, "You would wish to name him for the King— Richard?"

She looked down at the child, then flushed almost embarrassed. "I would rather he were John," she said quietly.

His expression was enigmatic. "As you wish," he replied, and left.

~≫— *Chapter Fourteen*

ALYS SMILED to herself as she peeped into the room off the hall which Elfrida had commandeered as a nursery. John de Courcelles was sleeping contentedly in his wooden cradle while Elfrida sat on a chair by his side, one foot rhythmically rocking his cradle. She looked up, as Alys stopped in the doorway, and held up one finger warningly. Most of the morning he had been fractious, demanding all her attention. Now at last she had lulled him off to slumber and she was anxious that he should not be disturbed. Alys allowed herself to be bullied by her nurse, and thankfully left him in her charge.

It was three months since they had returned to Birlstone and high summer. Already much had been done to set to rights the damage which had been done in the attack and to remedy the weeks of neglect which had followed. Walter, tired and dispirited, had been able to do little more than care for the horses and livestock, helped by one or two of the defenders. Now that the castle was once more fully manned, it had taken weeks of hard work to satisfy Sir Geoffrey. The prisoners taken in the attack had returned with them to Birlstone, and after months of being cooped up in the dungeons, fed on barely enough to keep body and soul together, they set to with gusto. The walls had now been repaired and the gatehouse and drawbridge reinforced. Outwardly, the castle showed little ill effects.

Since Sir Geoffrey had been extremely busy on the defences, Alys was determined to do her part. Elfrida and Sir Geoffrey had tried to keep her resting, but two weeks after the birth, found her superintending the cleansing of the keep, the laying of fresh rushes, hanging of new tapestries and a hundred and one household duties. Ibrahim made no comment. She seemed well enough. She delighted to ride to the village and talk again with her own people. Father Anselm had greeted her with tears of joy in his eyes. It had given him great happiness to baptise her infant son. The old man had feared for her, and honoured her that she had refused to remain behind the safety of her castle walls, and let village and church suffer the consequences of de Lacey's wrath.

She paused for a moment before crossing the bailey, as Rolf came across from the stables. She greeted him warmly. Sir Geoffrey had offered him the position of steward of Birlstone, but at first he had declined. He could not leave his men, he said. They had relied on him for so long, and he himself had become used to outlaw ways. Sir Geoffrey had shrugged lightly.

"As you wish, friend, but this life of yours cannot go on for ever. You are not growing younger, and the King's men will press you hardly. Those of your men who wish to join my service may do so. I shall ask no questions as to their past, if they will serve me. Think the matter over well."

Alys had regretted leaving him, when the second day after her child's birth, Ibrahim had pronounced her well enough to travel and she had accompanied Sir Geoffrey's force in a litter with Elfrida to cluck and fuss over her, as of old. One week later, Rolf had ridden up to the gatehouse with ten of his men; the rest had preferred to continue their lawless ways elsewhere. Gilbert had been no problem. On their return to Birlstone, he had been found missing. Walter, grim-lipped, had given a possible explanation.

"He was accused by the villagers of being in Sir William de Lacey's pay. When he walked through the manor, village men whispered after him, and I think he feared their black scowls. Anyway he disappeared and no one has been sorry."

Alys certainly was not and was relieved to see Rolf duly installed in his place. Oswin had become an archer in Sir Geoffrey's service. He was now a free yeoman and entitled to leave the manor if he so wished. It was unlikely that he would do so. He haunted the keep whenever he had a moment to spare, to peer down at the little heir, and Elfrida on more than one occasion angrily ordered him away, when she found him rousing the child from sleep, for the pleasure of seeing him gurgle and kick in sheer joy at living. No, Oswin was contented enough. He had been granted a small piece of land near the village and a cottage was to be built there to house his family. They could raise vegetables on their small plot, and Oswin had the right to graze their one cow and geese on the common land.

Since Elfrida was now fully occupied with the child, Alys had summoned his sister Marian, to work with her in the castle. The girl was a good worker and an accomplished needlewoman. When Alys saw her bend her young head over a tapestry frame, she experienced a pang of despair. In just such a position, had Blanchette sat, with the pale sun streaming from the slitted window onto her fair hair. Would she ever forget Blanchette? Rolf had made no reference to the death of his lovely daughter. Once or twice she had seen him stand by the spot of hallowed ground at the rear of the bailey, where they had lain her, his head uncovered, once in the driving rain. Sir Geoffrey passed no comment on his suspicions concerning de Lacey's death. One question Rolf would never be asked. It was better so.

Now Rolf seemed tired and a little harassed. For the first time, Alys was aware of unaccustomed hustle in the courtyard. She had been to the village early that morning, and had even now just peeped in at her small son.

"What is all this pother, Rolf? Do we expect visitors?"

"I have been searching for you, lady, but they told me you had gone to the village. Sir Geoffrey wishes to speak to you. He is in the hall."

She glanced round surprised, as four pack mules were led out from the stables and ostlers struggled with the refractory animals. Obviously some preparations of importance were afoot.

"Thank you, Rolf," she said quietly. "I will go to him."

Her heart beat quickened as she entered the keep again. It was always so when he summoned her. She saw so little of him. He had been so occupied with affairs and she told herself that it were wiser that for the time being, he should continue to sleep apart from her in her old chamber. She was now recovering from the ravages of childbirth. Her hair had regained its sheen and fell in silky brown waves to her waist. Her golden eyes were bright again, and she had taken pains with her appearance. He must notice her now, he *must*. She had given him his heart's delight. Surely he would spare her a part of his heart. She asked for no more. She had swallowed her disappointment at his continued courteous but withdrawn attitude to her. He sat with her at meal times, always asked after her welfare, delighted in a stolen hour in his son's company, but that was all. He had not touched her; in fact he had appeared to avoid her on occasions. She tried to convince herself that it was not so, but the hurt persisted. He disliked to be alone with her. The fact could not be denied. A little finger of fear touched her heart, when she paused in the entrance to the hall. He was seated at a trestle table, his head bent over some documents. She smiled at the familiar shorn locks. He had summoned the attentions of a barber on his return to Birlstone, and had cut his long fair hair, and had himself shaved the elegant golden beard. He was now as he had first been, that first day he had ridden to Birlstone well over a year ago. He looked up at once at her approach.

"Ah, there you are, my wife. I wished to see you before my departure. There are one or two matters I wish to discuss with you."

"Departure?" she faltered over the word and stood stock still.

"Yes. It is essential that a company be dispatched to Gwyndd to attend to affairs there. There is much to be done before the winter sets in. It seems wise for me to accompany them. I shall not be long. I promise I shall return before November. I am determined this time to spend Christmas with you and the child."

"You are like to be gone some months?"

"No more than three." He eyed her questioningly. "You need not fear. I shall leave you well guarded. I take only a company of men-at-arms. Roul shall ride with me, but I leave Alain Guilbert in charge and Walter is steady as a rock. Alain can be trusted. He will win his spurs next year. He knows my wishes regarding you."

She longed to say that surely Alain was trustworthy enough to lead the company to the Marches, but she bit back the words. He was determined, and it would profit her little. She sat down at his invitation, to study the accounts with him. She gave only half her attention, while he explained. He had laid in fresh supplies; the manor dues were gathered in. Rolf would superintend the Autumn slaughtering and salting of the meat. She need not concern herself.

"Ibrahim stays with you," he said as he rose. "I shall feel easier in my mind about both you and the boy if he remains here. He dislikes travelling. He prefers to concoct those evil tasting draughts of his in comfort. I shall go now up to my chamber to arm. You will excuse me."

"You go today?"

"At once. I ate a hasty meal while you were out. It is a fine day, and we can cover several miles before nightfall."

Her thoughts were chaotic as he left her. The blow had come so swiftly. He had not mentioned his intentions before. She could not believe that he would leave her again so soon. Only last night she had delighted in his company in the small garden he was having constructed in the bailey, for her pleasure. It was the fashion in France he said, to have such a pleasance as it was called. The serfs had dug up the earth and planted rose bushes and turf. Next year it would be finer, but even now it was pleasant in the sun to walk and imagine the future joy of cutting roses there. Her father had never thought to provide such a quiet place for her mother.

She got up abruptly. She could not stay here, or she would cry before the servants. She stumbled out of the hall, down the keep steps and across the bailey. She would go now to the garden. At this hour there would be no one there. Marian was busied storing away clean linen and the men were busy preparing for departure. She could be alone there with her grief. The little garden still looked rather bare and empty, but one or two roses had bloomed, and she pulled one from its stalk, disregarding the thorns which bloodied her fingers, and turning against the keep wall, which sheltered the flowers, burst into a storm of weeping. She was not conscious of time, but it was considerably later, that she felt a comforting arm round her shoulders and turned to cry against the cool silk of Ibrahim's robe. He had come to gather some rosemary leaves for a draught, and had been horrified to find her there. He let her cry on, then as the sobs grew less violent, he led her to a small wooden bench and drew her down on it.

"Come, lady, whatever ails you cannot be worth this," he said at last.

She lifted her head and miserably gulped back a final sob. "Oh, Ibrahim, I am sorry. I must look dreadful."

"Such weeping does not improve your appearance," he agreed smiling, "but the ravages can be repaired. Can you tell me what is wrong?"

"No," she looked beyond him to the battlements, already feeling somewhat foolish, "it is little enough. I am just a foolish woman. I become depressed sometimes, perhaps it is reaction."

He did not speak and she dropped her eyes, as he continued to look at her steadily. "You force me to confess. I am upset that he leaves me again so soon."

"He will not be long away."

"You think not?"

"I am sure of it."

"Ibrahim," she twisted a linen kerchief in her fingers, "at Gwyndd, had Sir Geoffrey . . . a . . . a woman who pleased him?"

His eyes twinkled. "He has not always lived as a monk."

"Then he goes back to some woman?"

"If you mean one woman in particular, certainly not."

Her tone was wistful. "His other castles must be much finer than Birlstone."

"Gwyndd is a defence fortress only, very bare and grim. It has nothing to recommend it but its position as a good stronghold on the border. His estate in Brittany is much more beautiful, but one day he will take you there and present you to his mother. She is a very autocratic old lady, and still very beautiful. They say she was the loveliest girl in all France when she was a bride."

"He must be very ashamed of me."

"Ashamed, what makes you say that, Lady Alys?"

She turned directly to face him, her chin tilted upwards in a brave gesture though her lips were trembling. "You know well enough what I mean, Ibrahim ben Echtal. I am clumsy and awkward and . . ."

"There is little trace of the limp now, excepting times when you are very wearied, but what of that? Sir Geoffrey noted you long ago, before I ever saw you or treated you. He wanted you then, why now should he change his mind?"

"De Lacey said that—but why, Ibrahim? Why

should he want a plain brown mouse such as I—and a cripple to boot?"

He stared at her blankly. "Brown mouse? By all the saints in your Christian calendar, can it be thus that you see yourself when you look in your mirror?"

"I don't understand . . ."

"Shall I tell you what I see, Lady Alys, before me now? I see a slim lovely girl with the most beautiful golden flecked eyes I have ever seen in my life, a flawless creamy skin and a proud carriage which befits a queen. You have a golden perfection seldom found in woman. Your native courage shines in your eyes, clear and direct, wonderfully honest, revealing one who never stoops to flattery or deceit. I tell you, child, I could make my fortune if I only had one such slave as you to sell in Damascus. What makes you belittle your beauty? Is it that you think Geoffrey prefers the pink and white daintiness of some court beauty, or the dark splendour of some southern French maid, over-ripe and early to age?"

"He spoke of me to you, before you came?"

"Indeed he did. Did I not tell you how he chose the material for you? When I beheld you, I was not disappointed."

"Then if he wants me—why does he leave me now?"

Ibrahim shook his head. "I do not know, Lady Alys, I can only surmise. He is concerned for you. When he returned to Winchester after wedding you, he was anxious to give you time to become accustomed to your married state. He sent me at once to tend you. Your frailty disturbed him and awakened his pity. He wished you to grow strong and happy; to take from you the responsibilities which had weighed you down too early; to see you laugh as you should have done in childhood. Then you quarrelled, and I know he was deeply ashamed that he had treated you badly. When he rode to Wales, he did not know of the child. He has blamed himself for your peril ever since. Was it that he forced you?"

"No, there was a bargain sealed between us. He had no cause to blame himself. I was ready enough to fulfil my part of it. Can he doubt that I regret the joy of holding my son in my arms?"

"There must have been some bad times at Mountsorrel."

"There were bad times, but not because of the child. When I thought I had lost Geoffrey, the thought of his coming was my only comfort."

"Nevertheless, I believe it is the fear of saddling you too soon with another child, which takes Geoffrey to Gwyndd now."

"But he has nought to fear. I am recovered. Oh, Ibrahim, I want babies—many more babies. He must see that."

"Then, Lady Alys, I suggest you inform him of the fact." She stared into his smiling eyes and drew back.

"I could not."

"Could not tell him you love him?"

"No, I could not."

"You western women are so odd. The women of my father's harem talked of nothing but their desire to please him. Here, you appear to want your lord to become your slave. I find this very strange."

"No, you are mistaken. I shall never attempt to bind Geoffrey to my side if he loves elsewhere. I should be happy with only a part of his heart. If he wishes to go, I shall not detain him." She rose to her feet, but she was now mistress of herself. "I thank you, Ibrahim. You have made me very happy. I have the courage now to await his return without complaining."

He watched her as she left the pleasance and crossed the bailey. He sighed, there was much he admired in this cold green land, and particularly its women, but he would never try to understand them.

Geoffrey was armed but for his helmet, when she entered the hall. He paused for a moment as she came up to him. It was thus she had first seen him, his mailed coif, thrust back, the sun glinting on his short fair hair. In spite of her brave determination to accept this parting with fortitude, she could not avoid tears springing to her eyes. She had lived empty and half-crazed through those bitter weeks, when she had thought him lost to her. Would her life consist of nothing but his gentle concern and these interminable absences? Hardly knowing what she said, she bent and took his hand. "Please, Geoffrey, take me with you."

He stooped and grasped her shoulders. "Little one, I tell you again, there is naught to fear. You will be safe here."

"Geoffrey, I don't want to be safe, I want to be with you."

A pulse beat in his throat though she could not see it, hidden as it was, by his chain mail. He swallowed hard.

"My dear, the journey is long and hard and Gwyndd comfortless. I cannot but think you will be happier here with the child."

She drew away from him and tilted her chin proudly. "If I am continually to be neglected so, I had better know it now. I have borne you a son. Is that all you wished from me? Tell me honestly, and I will accept it."

He looked back at her, amazed. "You make too much of this parting. How can you accuse me of neglect? I have done everything for your comfort."

"Everything but stay with me. How can I bear you more heirs if I live always alone?"

He forced his tone to sound even. "There will be time later for more children."

"Geoffrey, I want them now, while I am young. Will you look at me. I am strong and fit, not some weakling. Was it a fragile flower who directed the defence of Birlstone and came with you from Mountsorrel?"

He drew her suddenly into his arms and tilted up her chin with one firm hand. "Aye, and I shall never forgive myself. You could have died there, in that hut of Rolf's of a child I had forced on you."

"Geoffrey, do you love me?" Her muffled whisper came to him and he caught her close. She smelt the de-

cided male smell of leather harness and her tender skin
was bruised by the steel links of his heavy chain mail,
but she gloried in his nearness.

"Love you?" he questioned huskily. "I loved you
from the second I saw your child's face looking out
from its brown hood in a little silversmith's shop in
Nottingham. You were with your father and he bought
you some trumpery trinket. I could never forget you
from that moment. Since I did not know him, I made
enquiries at court, planning to strike an acquaintance
and discover whether or not you had yet been
promised or given in marriage, but I found he had
stayed only a little time and taken you back with him.
The Prince claimed my duty and it was not until I met
your father again, last year at the jousts, that I had any
opportunity to seek you out. I planned to return with
him and give you time to know me. Oh yes, he spoke
of you often, but he was over occupied with his courtship of some wealthy widow in the town. When he was
killed, I gave way to temptation and begged your hand
of the Prince, which he willingly granted."

Held close in his arms, she listened with a kind of
wonder. "When I saw you, I knew I had been unfair,
but, Alys, I had no time to woo you. There were others
who coveted Birlstone, and I had to secure your safety,
but it seemed you hated me and deplored the system
which had given you as a chattel into my hands. I
swore I would wait for your love to kindle but jealousy
of de Lacey drove me to take you before you were
ready—and it almost cost you your life. You ask me if
I want you. Look at me, look at my eyes. Don't you
know that if I stay here I may put you in fresh peril. I
make myself go until Christmas, for if I stay, it must be
as your husband. Try to understand and be patient."

"But I do understand, Geoffrey." She drew herself
firmly away. Tears were still staining her cheeks, but
happiness shone in her eyes. "Oh my love, I can wait
now. Go—go from me now. I will stay here. Do not
ask me to bid you a formal farewell from the gate-
house. I could not bear that—but swear that you will

come before Christmas. Your son and I will be here then waiting for you."

He made to approach her again, but she gestured him away. He hesitated once, then turned and left her. She heard the ring of his spurs on the stone steps and moved to the window. It was too high for her to see him emerge from the keep and she sank down on a wooden bench, since her knees were trembling. When she heard the sound of the cavalcade moving out across the drawbridge, she gave a little sigh, then sat on perfectly still.

When she heard steps again ascending the stairs, she rose, half expecting Alain. Geoffrey stood in the door-way, still mailed, but he had removed his steel gaunt-lets and he held out his arms and waited. She choked back a sob and sped across the hall. He lifted her off her feet and crushed his mouth on hers. She clung to him until she felt her breath would cease. Afterwards, he sat in the carved chair with her in his arms, her head against his breast.

"It seemed," he said quietly, "a poor time to make the journey. Campaigning cannot begin again until the Spring and Roul will do my part as well as I."

So many months before the Spring and then perhaps she would go with him. A little secret smile played round her lips as she realised it might not be possible. For the first time in her life, Alys wished for the long-est and hardest winter Birlstone had ever known.